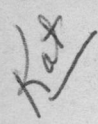

THE KILLING SWARM

So intent were the pair of gunmen on catching Morning Flower that they did not notice Skye Fargo right away. One of them glanced toward the horses, but Fargo was on the ground on the far side and escaped scrutiny. Pushing erect, Fargo drew the Colt. He started to step around the stallion and nearly fell on his face when his numb feet refused to do as he wanted them to. Grabbing his saddle to keep from going down, he steadied himself.

Morning Flower was as fleet as a doe. She held her own for a few seconds as she bounded gracefully across the meadow. Then the horses gained on her, converging from the right and the left, the killers whooping and laughing. Their lecherous expressions left no doubt as to what they had in mind.

Fargo extended his arm over the pinto. Cocking the hammer, he aimed just as the man he was going to shoot spotted him. . . .

THE TRAILSMAN
#177

COLORADO WOLFPACK

by

Jon Sharpe

A SIGNET BOOK

SIGNET
Published by the Penguin Group
Penguin Books USA Inc., 375 Hudson Street,
New York, New York 10014, U.S.A.
Penguin Books Ltd, 27 Wrights Lane,
London W8 5TZ, England
Penguin Books Australia Ltd, Ringwood,
Victoria, Australia
Penguin Books Canada Ltd, 10 Alcorn Avenue,
Toronto, Ontario, Canada M4V 3B2
Penguin Books (N.Z.) Ltd, 182-190 Wairau Road,
Auckland 10, New Zealand

Penguin Books Ltd, Registered Offices:
Harmondsworth, Middlesex, England

First published by Signet, an imprint of Dutton Signet,
a division of Penguin Books USA Inc.

First Printing, September, 1996
10 9 8 7 6 5 4 3 2 1

The first chapter of this book originally appeared in *Curse of the Grizzly*, the one hundred seventy-sixth volume in this series.

 REGISTERED TRADEMARK—MARCA REGISTRADA

Printed in the United States of America

The Trailsman

Beginnings . . . they bend the tree and they mark the man. Skye Fargo was born when he was eighteen. Terror was his midwife, vengeance his first cry. Killing spawned Skye Fargo, ruthless, cold-blooded murder. Out of the acrid smoke of gunpowder still hanging in the air, he rose, cried out a promise never forgotten.

The Trailsman they began to call him all across the West: searcher, scout, hunter, the man who could see where others only looked, his skills for hire but not his soul, the man who lived each day to the fullest, yet trailed each tomorrow. Skye Fargo, the Trailsman, and the seeker who could take the wildness of a land and the wanting of a woman and make them his own.

*1861—Southwest Colorado Territory,
where the peaks touch the sky,
the women are willing,
and lead flies thick and fast.*

1

Few things can get a man's attention faster than having the business end of a gun jammed into the base of his spine.

One moment Skye Fargo was strolling along a rutted dirt track that passed between two short rows of tents and cabins, the next a bulky form sprang out of the darkness and a pistol was shoved into the small of his back. Instantly, the big man froze.

"This is a warning, friend," declared a voice that reminded Fargo of gravel rattling down a slope. "If you know what's good for you, you'll quit asking questions about that old coot, McDermott. Savvy?"

Fargo knew better, but he could not help saying, "The last I heard, this is a free country, mister. I can do what I damn well please."

"You can if you want to die."

The back of Fargo's skull exploded in searing pain. His legs buckled and he sagged to his knees, struggling to stay conscious. No attempt was made to strip him of his Colt, but a hand did knock his hat off and roughly grab him by the hair. His head was snapped back. He caught a whiff of foul breath laced with liquor.

"This was your only warning, jackass," his attacker growled into his ear. "Keep on poking around and you'll be pushing up fireweed come spring."

A boot slammed into Fargo's kidney, adding to his agony. He slumped onto his elbows as footsteps rapidly sped into the night. The only other sounds were the nicker of a horse at a hitchrack, and tinny music from the ramshackle excuse for a saloon farther down the street.

Fargo did not stay bent over for long. Gritting his teeth

against the torment, he straightened, reclaimed his white hat, and slowly stood. For a few seconds the world spun and wobbled as if it were a kid's top, then his piercing lake-blue eyes cleared. He slapped dust from his buckskins with his hat, placed it on his head, and headed for the saloon, his anger mounting with every stride.

The town, if such it could be called, wasn't on any map. It had sprung up within the past six months as miners, settlers, and others started flocking deep into the Rocky Mountains from points east.

Some folks called it Pfeifferville, others San Juan, still others Pagosa Springs in honor of the hot mineral springs nearby. It was located high in the Colorado Rockies. The San Juan Mountains surrounded it on three sides. To the northeast reared the Continental Divide.

It was as remote a place as a man was likely to find anywhere. There was no marshal or sheriff or lawman of any kind, not even a justice of the peace. If someone were wronged, they had to take the matter into their own hands or turn the other cheek.

Fargo wasn't the forgiving sort. Pausing, he pulled his Colt, flipped open the loading gate, and made sure he had five beans in the wheel, as a Texan might say. He twirled the pistol back into his holster and walked on. Ahead, he noticed a patch of ground at the corner of the whiskey mill. Thanks to lantern light spilling through the only window, he saw something that brought a grim smile to his mouth.

The saloon did not have batwing doors. In fact, there wasn't a door of any kind. The owner, an Irishman named Sullivan, was too lazy to make one and too cheap to have one shipped in. He merely tacked a blanket over the opening every night before turning in and took it down the next day. Since everyone knew that he slept on the bar with a scattergun cradled in his arms, no one tried to help themselves to his stock.

On this particular night the saloon was crowded. Smoke hung heavy in the air. So did the odor of alcohol and sweat. Jumbled voices rose to the rafters.

Fargo stepped to the right with his back to the log wall as soon as he entered. His thumbs hooked in his gunbelt, he let his eyes adjust to the glare. No one paid much attention to him. Men were drinking, gambling, or joking with the two fallen doves who worked for Sullivan. He studied the feet of everyone in sight. Most wore boots. A few favored moccasins. Only two men in the whole establishment had on store-bought shoes.

When he did not find what he was looking for, Fargo sidled along the wall, passing a table where four men played five card stud. A grizzled character holding his cards close to his chest glanced up sharply, as if he suspected Fargo of trying to peek at his hand.

"Hey, you there!" he said gruffly, his right cheek crammed with chewing tobacco, his face looking swollen. "I don't like anyone standin' behind me when I'm playin'."

Fargo had stopped to study the footwear of the men at the bar. A beefy character at the very end caught his interest. The man had just been given a whiskey and was raising the glass. He was going to go on but fingers plucked at his sleeve.

"I don't like bein' ignored, stranger," the card player snapped. An old Dragoon Army Model revolver was wedged under his wide brown belt, and he put a hand on the butt. "Give me one good reason why I shouldn't get up out of this chair and teach you some manners."

Some of the other men snickered.

Fargo looked the cantankerous cuss right in the eyes. "I can think of one."

"Oh? Let me hear it."

Lowering his hand near his Colt, Fargo said in a flat tone, "You can't finish the game if you're dead."

The man reddened and started to rise. He even began to draw the Dragoon. But the next moment he stopped. His brow wrinkled. He chewed on his lower lip a few seconds while staring at Fargo's gun hand. When he looked back up at Fargo's face, he swallowed hard and said softly, "You have a good point. So let's not do anything hasty." He mustered a grin and shrugged. "No hard feelings, I hope? When I have too much red-eye in me, my mouth tends to get the better of my brain."

Fargo went on, circling the room to come up on the customer at the bar from the rear. He threaded past several tables and was skirting the last one when a heavenly figure in a tight red dress materialized in front of him. Full lips the same color quirked upward, revealing teeth as white as pearls. Fragrant perfume tingled his nose.

"Howdy, handsome," the dove greeted him. "I'm Marcy. Care to treat me to some conversation fluid and chew the cud a spell?" Her warm hand fell on his. "I can make it well worth your while, if you take my meaning."

It had been over a week since Fargo last enjoyed the company of a lovely, willing female. He was strongly tempted. But the knot on the back of his noggin reminded him that he had an account to settle. "Maybe later," he said.

Marcy did not hide her disappointment. "Suit yourself. I just hope I'm still available." She gave his cheek a playful squeeze. "I like gents with broad shoulders and narrow hips. They always have a lot of stamina."

"No one has ever complained about how long I stay in the saddle," Fargo quipped.

"I don't doubt it for a minute." Winking, Marcy sashayed off, her bosom close to bursting at the seams.

Fargo took two more paces and planted himself. He was now less than six feet from the man at the end of the bar, who kept gazing toward the entrance as if expecting someone. Cracking his voice like a whip to be heard above the general din, Fargo called out, "Turn, bastard, and face me."

All talk ceased. Glasses stopped tinkling, poker chips stopped clattering. All eyes turned toward the big man in buckskins.

The beefy customer at the bar had stiffened. Slowly setting down his glass, he pivoted. His features were as flinty as quartz, his eyes as shifty as quicksand. Stubble covered a grimy chin. He wore a flannel shirt and dirty jeans. Strapped around his waist was a long-barreled Remington. "Are you talking to me?" he demanded.

Fargo nodded. "I thought maybe you'd like to try and slug me again, only this time my back won't be turned."

A few patrons commenced whispering among themselves. The man at the counter licked his thick lips, then declared, "I don't know what the hell you're talking about, mister. I never saw you before in my life."

"You're a liar."

All those standing near the beefy man suddenly wanted to be somewhere else. Pushing and shoving, they cleared a wide space around him.

Sullivan, the proprietor, hurried down the bar, waving a dirty cloth in alarm. "See here, fellows!" he said. "I don't know what's going on, but I don't like gunplay in my establishment. Too many bottles get busted. You'll have to take your grudge outdoors."

Fargo had no intention of moving. He waited, poised, for the man at the bar to make his move. "Don't try to deny it was you," he said. "You're wearing the proof."

"I don't know what you're talking about," the man testily insisted.

Without taking his eyes off him, Fargo addressed the barkeep. "Sullivan, did you empty a spittoon out front a couple of minutes ago?"

"Two of them," the proprietor said. "Why?"

"Somebody just jumped me," Fargo explained. "Whoever it was hit me over the head from behind, then ran in here, figuring he could lose himself in the crowd."

More muttering broke out.

Sullivan had stopped shy of the thickset character. "And you're claiming it was Jenkins, here? That's a powerful accusation. What makes you suspect him?"

"He's the only one with tobacco juice all over the lower half of his boots," Fargo replied. He expected Jenkins to go on denying it, to argue the point a while. Instead, the man cursed and made a grab for the Remington. In a blur the pistol flashed up and out, but as quick as Jenkins was, Fargo proved faster. The first blast of the Colt rocked Jenkins on his heels. The second blast smashed him back against the bar where he triggered two wild shots that gouged into the ceiling. Fargo's third and final shot was smack between the eyes.

Jenkins oozed to the floor like so much limp clay. The Remington thudded at his feet and he wound up falling across it, blank astonishment lining his face. His body twitched briefly and was still.

No one else moved. Gunsmoke curled from the end of the Colt as Fargo advanced to verify the man was dead. He would rather have questioned Jenkins before resorting to his six-shooter, but it couldn't be helped. Leaning an elbow on the bar, he replaced the spent cartridge while watching the other patrons carefully in case Jenkins had friends among them. The talk and card play resumed. Most went on about their business, giving him a wide berth.

Sullivan came over. "Hell's bells, mister. You haven't been in this two-bit rat hole two hours, and look at what you've done! That was some mighty slick shooting, if I do say so my own self."

Fargo had stopped at the saloon earlier to wash the dust of the trail from his dry throat, then gone off to find a bite to eat. It had been on his way back that the man named Jenkins had caught him by surprise. He nudged the body with a toe. "You knew this snake in the grass?"

"No better than I do most of my customers," the Irishman said. "Sure, he came in here a lot since he turned up about two months ago. But he wasn't a talkative gent. All I can tell you is that he had a mean streak a mile wide, and that he rode with Wolf Rollins."

"Who?"

Sullivan leaned over the counter to speak quietly. "It's not a name I want to repeat twice out loud. He has ears everywhere, and he can sling lead as fast as you can, friend, if not faster. I'd stay well clear of him, were I you." The bartender looked both ways before going on. "They say Rollins is from North Carolina. He's a big, tough bruiser who showed up in the Springs shortly after word of Ike McDermott's silver find leaked out."

McDermott. Fargo had overheard a pair of faro players jawing about the prospector during his first visit to the saloon. Curiosity had sparked him to ask a few questions, which Jenkins must have overheard. "Is it true that McDermott struck it rich somewhere in these mountains?"

Sullivan wiped a spot of blood off the counter. "That's the rumor. But so far the only silver old Ike has shown anyone is that incredibly huge piece of ore those two fellows told you about a while ago, and a few smaller ones."

"You saw the big one?"

"With my own peepers," the bartender confirmed. "It must have weighed ten pounds, if it weighed an ounce. Pure silver, clean through. Ike brought it in and plunked it down on the bar, right over there." Sullivan pointed. "He treated everyone to a round, and bragged on how he would soon be the richest man in the country, richer even than John Jacob Astor."

Fargo was skeptical. He'd heard such boasts before. After laboring long and hard to strike it rich, a man would find a few nuggets and let it go to his head. "Was it the drink talking, or do you think he really hit the mother lode?"

Sullivan chuckled. "With old Ike, it's hard to say. He does like to run on at the mouth. Still, I've never seen him drink more than he can handle. And I've never heard of him telling a lie."

It wasn't difficult for Fargo to put two and two together. Word of McDermott's find had spread far and wide, luring those who favored the shady side of the law, men like Wolf Rollins and those who rode with him. Men who would stop at nothing to learn where the prospector had made his strike. "Those faro players told me that McDermott is having a hard time of it," he mentioned.

"So I've heard, but old Ike hasn't been by here in weeks so I don't know if the stories are true," Sullivan said, coming around the end of the bar. Placing his hands on his hips, he clucked like an irate hen. "Will you look at all that blood! And I'll have to clean it up!"

"What stories?" Fargo asked as the proprietor stooped to slip his hands under Jenkins's arms.

Sullivan started dragging the corpse toward a door at the back. "That Wolf Rollins and his wild bunch are making life miserable for McDermott. They won't rest until they find out where he struck the vein." Sullivan grunted and slowed to add, "A week or so ago they jumped him on his way here. He got away but they shot a pack horse of his. A month or so ago, it was an old mongrel he was fond of."

"It sounds as if McDermott could use a helping hand," Fargo remarked, trailing along.

"Maybe so, but you won't find anyone in these parts loco enough to buck Wolf Rollins. He has eight or nine gunsharks working for him. Curly wolves, the whole outfit." Sullivan took a firmer hold. "They'd as soon shoot anyone who meddled in their business as look at them. Mark my words, mister. If you're thinking what I think you're thinking, you could wind up six feet under."

"Jenkins said the same thing," Fargo said.

"Jenkins was a kitten compared to Wolf Rollins," Sullivan noted, and nodded at the door.

Fargo held it open. After the barkeep and the dead man had gone on through, he returned to the bar. By rights the McDermott business was none of his affair. He didn't know the man. He had no personal stake in the clash. So the smart thing to do would be to mount up and ride out in the morning. But it galled him, being threatened by one of Rollins's men just because he had asked a few innocent questions. No one ran roughshod over him. Ever.

"A penny for your thoughts, handsome."

The tantalizing aroma of perfume told Fargo who was behind him. Marcy's fingertips delicately stroked his ear before settling on his shoulder and caressing his neck. "Can I treat you to a drink?"

"Do bears like honey?" The brunette brushed against him as she stepped up. "I'm afraid there are two things in this world I can't do without. One is good sipping whiskey."

"And the other?"

Like a horse fancier sizing up a thoroughbred, Marcy ran her eyes up and down his powerful frame. She focused on a point several inches below his belt and said huskily, "If you can't guess, you don't deserve to buy me that drink." Her hand strayed to his chest. "I have high hopes for you, big man. Don't disappoint me."

Fargo's laughter seemed to put many of the other customers more at ease. The hubbub became louder, much as it had been before he shot Jenkins. "I'll do my best," he promised.

Over the course of half an hour, Fargo heard her life

story. How she had been raised in Ohio and moved west weeks after marrying a fool who thought the two of them could cross the prairie alone. How Cheyenne Indians had shown him the error of his ways. How she had been traded to whiskey peddlers, who took her to Denver. She had decided to head for San Francisco but somehow or other had wound up in Pagosa Springs and now was scraping together enough money to finish the trip.

Similar tales of woe were commonplace. Fargo had listened to more of them than he could count during his wide-flung travels. It was added proof, if any was needed, that the frontier was no place for greenhorns and amateurs. The wilderness was a harsh mistress. It broke the spirit of those too weak to meet it on its own terms. It crushed those who could not cope. In the wild, only the fittest survived, whether they were deer, buffalo, or humans.

"What about you, big man?" Marcy was saying. "What do you do for a living?"

"Some scouting, some tracking, whatever interests me at the moment," Fargo said, seeing no need to be more specific.

They had moved to a table. Marcy contrived to lean forward so that her ample breasts almost spilled from her dress. "What about now? Why are you in the Springs?"

"I'm just passing through."

"That's all?"

Fargo was about to take a swallow of whiskey. Something in the way she asked made him look at her, but she was smiling sweetly so he thought nothing of it. "I never stay in any one place very long," he said. Finishing his drink, he fished in a pocket for coins to pay the Irishman. At that moment a pair of burly hard cases entered. He knew their kind well. They reminded him of coyotes on the prowl, and he automatically lowered his right hand under the table as they surveyed the room. Side by side they stepped to a table and engaged a skinny card player in conversation.

Marcy had also noticed them. "Oh, no," she declared nervously.

"What's wrong?"

"Those two ride with Wolf Rollins. The one with the scar on his jaw is Bob Hackett. The other man is Fess Webster. They're Southerners. From what I hear tell, they were chased out of every state south of the Mason Dixon for one crime or another before they hooked up with Wolf." She fortified herself with a healthy dose of coffin varnish. "They were good friends with Jenkins. I don't imagine they'll take kindly to him being gunned down."

As if to accent her point, the pair turned toward them. Both glowered at Fargo, then spread out to approach him. Marcy promptly rose and moved back out of harm's way. Fargo, using his left hand, poured another shot and made a point of placing the bottle off to one side so it would not be in the line of fire if he had to unlimber the Colt on the spur of the moment. He faced the two men when they were still a good eight feet away and said firmly, "That's far enough."

Hackett and Webster halted. They traded glances and the one with the scar began to ease his hand toward his Colt.

"Do that, and Jenkins won't be the only one planted tomorrow," Fargo warned.

In the second silence that gripped the saloon since Fargo's arrival, Bob Hackett rested a scuffed black boot on an empty chair and puffed up his chest. "We ride for Wolf Rollins," he stated, as if the statement alone would make Fargo quake in fear.

"It's a rare hombre who will brag about being close friends with a polecat," Fargo responded. Outwardly, he was the perfect picture of total calm. Inwardly, he was coiled to draw or strike out or do whatever else the occasion might demand should they come at him.

Webster made a sound reminiscent of a riled rattler. "You've got quite a mouth on you, buckskin. Maybe it's time someone closed it for you, permanent-like."

Fargo's smile was masterful. It mocked them and insulted them at the same time. "Care to try?"

Without another word the pair wheeled and stalked into the night. A collective sigh was let out by half the men in the saloon. Sullivan appeared, shaking his head. "I've never met anyone with the knack you have for making enemies.

I'd wager you even tussled with the midwife who delivered you."

Grinning, Fargo paid and looked for Marcy. To his surprise, she was nowhere to be seen. He nodded at the proprietor and left. Not taking any chances, he stepped quickly to the side once he passed through the door and stood in the shadows a while to satisfy himself that no one lay in ambush. Several minutes went by before he headed west down the street.

Fargo figured that the incident was over, that he could retrieve his stallion and go find a nice quiet spot to bed down for the night. But he figured wrong. For as he came abreast of the next building, he heard a telltale swishing sound above him. He tried to duck and jump aside, but it was too late.

A noose dropped down over his head.

2

In the blink of an eye the rope was yanked hard from above, constricting the noose around Skye Fargo's neck so tight that the manila hemp gouged deep into his flesh. He was jerked upward until only the toes of his boots brushed the ground.

Most anyone else, especially pilgrims from east of the Mississippi who had hardly ever set eyes on a rope much less used one, would have panicked and grabbed for the noose in an attempt to pry it loose. Fargo knew better. Skilled ropers made their slip knots so well that no one could untie one before being strangled. So he clutched at the rope *above* the knot, instead, and tugged with all his strength. It lowered him an inch or two, enough to partially plant himself and catch a ragged breath.

It was well he did. For out of the darkness rushed Fess Webster, a wicked bowie knife glinting dully in the pale light from the saloon. His smile was equally wicked. Without uttering a sound, he closed in and slashed.

Fargo had to hand it to them. It was a clever way to dispose of someone. But he was not about to go down without a fight. As the blade sheared the crisp air toward his chest, he twisted to the right, swept his right foot up, and caught Webster on the knee.

There was a muffled pop. Webster uttered a low growl of mingled anguish and outrage. Stumbling backward, he recovered, then attacked again. But this time he limped, and he was much more wary.

The rope was given a harder yank than ever. Evidently Bob Hackett was trying to help his pard out by keeping their intended victim off balance.

It almost worked. Fargo tottered and would have lost his footing had he not collided with the building and been able to brace his back against the log wall. His breath had been choked off, but he could still defend himself, so he did, dodging a thrust at his vitals and arcing his left boot into Webster's groin.

Webster shifted at the last instant, sparing himself the brunt of the kick. Still, he doubled over, clasped his privates, and shuffled a few feet to one side, his face as red as a beet.

Fargo tugged again. The rope would not give. He fought for air but could not inhale. Already his chest hurt terribly as his lungs strained for relief. Hiking his right leg, he drove a hand under the top of his boot. His fingers closed on the smooth hilt of his Arkansas toothpick, snug in its ankle sheath. Drawing the slender knife, he elevated his arm and cut at the rope, sawing in a frenzy, aware that unless he freed himself quickly, he had mere seconds to live.

Webster had straightened. The color had faded from his cheeks. "You damn bastard!" he snarled, and struck once more, savagely, spearing the bowie at Fargo's throat. This time he was not to be denied.

Fargo had other ideas, even though he had not yet severed the rope all the way. Desperately pivoting, he felt a twinge of pain as the bowie nicked his side. In the same split second, he flashed the toothpick downward into Webster's wrist. Blood spurted. The hard case let out a yelp and frantically back-pedaled, covering the pumping wound with his left hand.

There wasn't a moment to lose. Again Fargo applied the toothpick to the rope, just as Hackett redoubled his own effort. Fargo's feet came clear off the ground. His vision swam, and he thought that his chest would burst. Then the rope parted. He fell and swayed. If not for the wall, he would have pitched onto his face.

A few heaving breaths were enough to relieve Fargo's lungs. He could see clearly again, and he was mildly surprised to find Fess Webster bolting like a jackrabbit toward a gap between a cabin and a tent on the other side of the rutted track. In a twinkling Fargo transferred the toothpick to his other hand and palmed the Colt.

Ordinarily Fargo did not shoot his enemies in the back, but Webster merited an exception. He brought the Colt up, sighting for a clean shot between the shoulder blades. Before he could squeeze the trigger, however, something landed heavily on his head and shoulders. It was the rope, dropped by Hackett to buy time for Webster to escape. It blocked Fargo's vision and entangled his arm just long enough to get the job done. By the time he tore the coils off him, the killer with the bowie was gone.

Fargo took three strides and whirled, training the Colt on the spot where Bob Hackett had been. Only Hackett wasn't there. He ran to the side of the building where wooden crates had been stacked high enough for a man to reach the roof and scrambled up them. As he poked his head above the rim he glimpsed a flurry of movement at the rear. He heard a thud. Vaulting up, he ran to the back and spied a furtive figure vanishing into the underbrush.

It would be useless to give chase. All Hackett had to do was lie low and blaze away when Fargo showed himself. Reluctantly, the big man turned back and descended. He rubbed his raw throat as he walked to where his hat had fallen. Holstering the Colt, he put the hat back on. The toothpick went into its sheath.

A gleam of light on metal drew Fargo to the middle of the street. Fess Webster had dropped his knife. Fargo picked it up and hefted the heavy weapon made famous by Jim Bowie, hero of the Alamo, years ago. A few times in the past he had toyed with the notion of toting one himself. The blade was wide enough and thick enough to gut a grizzly, and the hilt thick enough to crack a man's skull.

Suddenly slight footsteps alerted Fargo to someone behind him. Spinning, he snapped the bowie up to throw. Just in time he saw who it was.

Marcy gasped and retreated a step. "It's me!" she bleated. "I didn't mean to startle you!"

Fargo lowered the knife and tucked it under his belt. "You could get yourself killed, coming up on a man like that in the dark," he warned.

"Sorry," the brunette apologized. Sashaying over to him, she took his arm and pretended to pout. "Is this the thanks a girl gets for traipsing after you?" Her gaze darted to the bowie. "Where did you get that big old knife, anyhow?"

"It was a gift," Fargo said, and let it go at that. He didn't like standing out there in the open, not when Hackett or Webster might take it into their heads to double back and take up where they had left off, using a rifle instead of a rope. Which reminded him. Fargo steered Marcy to the building and helped himself to the one Hackett had dropped. Looping it, he headed down the street, staying close to the buildings.

"What was that doing just lying there?" Marcy asked. "Is it yours?"

"It is now," Fargo said. Sliding the coils over his shoulder, he scoured the pitiful excuse for a town from one end to the other. It was as quiet as a cemetery.

"I went to fetch my shawl, and when I came back, you were gone," Marcy said. She pressed her warm body against him, purring. "Here I thought you might like to spend the night with me. I have a small place out back of the saloon. It's not much, but it's private."

Fargo almost turned her down. He was tired from a long day on the trail and wanted time to himself to think through the whole McDermott business and what he was going to do about Wolf Rollins. But a familiar twitching in his loins reminded him of how long it had been since last he savored the company of a frisky young filly. "We have to get my horse. Then I'm all yours."

Marcy giggled and squeezed his arm. "I can hardly wait, handsome. Something tells me this will be a night to long remember."

The Ovaro dozed at a rickety hitchrack in front of a huge canvas tent. A sign proudly proclaimed the tent to be the only dry goods store between Denver and Tucson. Fargo knew that wasn't the case, but he hadn't quibbled with the elderly owner when the man sold him a box of ammo for his rifle shortly after he arrived.

"Goodness gracious!" Marcy exclaimed, admiring the Ovaro. "What a magnificent animal."

The pinto stallion stood well over fifteen hands high. Its coat was lustrous, its mane and tail long and full. Anyone who knew anything about horses could tell at a glance that it was built for speed and endurance. It had served Fargo in good stead as he traveled the country from one end to the other. He owed it his life more times than he cared to count, and he would sooner part with an arm or leg than with the stallion.

The Ovaro lifted its head. Fargo patted its neck and scratched behind its ears before unwrapping the reins. Holding them in his left hand, he said to Marcy, "Lead the way."

Her place turned out to be a small shack located no more than twenty yards from the rear of the saloon. Another shack, a dozen yards to the east, was home to the other dove who worked for Sullivan.

Between the two was a wide tract of lush grass. Fargo took a picket pin from his saddlebags and tethered the stallion, then stripped off his saddle and blanket and carried both inside.

Marcy had lit a lantern. The single room was small but tidy. It boasted an old worn bed, a small woodstove, a chest of drawers and a table barely big enough for two people to use at the same time. "All the comforts of home," Marcy said self-consciously. "Sorry it's not fancier."

"I've slept in worse," Fargo said to put her at ease. Depositing his gear in a corner, he pulled the Henry from his boot and leaned the big rifle against the wall near the bed so it would be handy if Hackett and Webster paid them a visit. The sight of a shelf laden with canned goods, flour, and a loaf of bread made his mouth water.

Marcy noticed his expression. "Are you hungry?"

"Starved," Fargo admitted. The puny portions of venison and potatoes he'd had for supper had hardly whetted his appetite.

"Then why don't I fix you vittles before we settle in," she offered, and Fargo did not object. In short order she had a fire crackling in the stove and a pot of coffee boiling. She also made a batch of biscuits. A delicious aroma filled the shack, causing his stomach to rumble so loud that she laughed. "You weren't kidding, were you?" Flipping a biscuit, she said, "Have a seat. It won't be long."

Fargo eased into a chair. The warmth and the food and the pleasure of her company drained the tension from his whipcord frame. For the first time since leaving California, he allowed himself to relax completely. It was a rare luxury. On the trail, a man had to be on his guard every minute of every day. Hostiles, wild beasts, and outlaws were a constant menace. In the towns he passed through it wasn't much better. There were always sidewinders like Jenkins, Hackett, and Webster to watch out for.

The biscuits tasted as wonderful as they smelled. Fargo smothered seven of them in butter. Every bite melted in his mouth. He washed them down with four steaming hot cups of black coffee. When he was done, he leaned back and rubbed his stomach in content. "I'm obliged."

Marcy sat across from him, sipping Arbuckle's. "Sorry I didn't have a slab of steak or stew."

"Quit apologizing so much," Fargo said. "You don't have to answer to anyone about the way you live except yourself. If you're happy, it's all that matters."

The brunette blinked a few times. "No one ever put it quite that way before." Reaching out, she gently covered his hand with hers. "I like you, handsome. Like you a lot." She paused. "Wouldn't it be nice if we were to go to San Francisco together? Think of it. Just the two of us. What a grand time we could have!"

Disappointment gripped Fargo. He suspected that she was as desperate to get out of the situation she was in as he had been to get out of that noose. Since he didn't know her very well, he had no way of knowing if she was the type who would use her body to entice someone gullible enough to do as she wanted. If that were the case, she was in for a disappointment of her own. He bent his will to no one, man or woman.

"I'm on my way east, not west," Fargo made plain. "If all you're looking for is someone to hook up with, I'm not the one you want. I might as well leave now and spare you any grief."

Marcy recoiled as if he had slapped her on the cheek. "You're not one to mince words, are you?"

"No."

She regarded him intently a few moments. "I can't say I'm not a trifle upset, but I do thank you for your honesty. Most men would have taken advantage of me, then gone their merry way not giving a damn about my feelings."

Fargo downed the last of the coffee in his tin cup. "So what will it be?" he bluntly demanded. "Do I stay, or do I go?"

The brunette never hesitated. "I'd be awful put out if you were to leave. It's been a coon's age since I was last with a man I actually wanted to be with. I'm looking forward to this."

"Prove it," Fargo challenged her.

A seductive smile creased Marcy's rosy mouth as she slowly rose. She held herself so that her breasts swelled the fabric covering them. Her hips wriggled invitingly as she came around the table. "I see that gleam in your eyes," she teased. "You're hungry for a lot more than food."

"I never claimed any different." Fargo stared at her alluring bosom, at her narrow waist, and the shapely contours of her thighs outlined under her dress. His loins twitched as they had before.

Marcy halted beside the chair. "Well, what are you waiting for? Here's your dessert."

Looping an arm around her waist, Fargo pulled her even closer. She cooed in surprised delight as he nuzzled the junction of her thighs, pressing deep between them to her core. Marcy parted her legs to allow him more room, and he stroked her from front to back with the bridge of his nose. She quivered while running her fingers through his hair, knocking his hat off in the process.

"Why, Skye, I do declare!" she said. "I never took you to be so frisky!"

Pulling back, Fargo grinned. "You haven't seen anything yet." Suddenly rising, he scooped her into his arms and whirled her in a complete circle. Then, striding to the bed, he set her flat on her back.

Marcy's rich brunette locks formed a brown halo around

her sultry features. She formed an oval with her lips and poked the red tip of her tongue out. Her body squirmed, her hips giving tiny thrusts, hints of the ecstasy to come. "I'm all yours, handsome," she said in a husky voice.

The dress had slipped around her waist, revealing her silken thighs and her white underthings. Fargo could not take his eyes off those thighs. They were as fine a pair as he had ever seen, and so smooth to the touch that he would have sworn he was stroking glass.

At the first contact of his fingers, Marcy shivered as if cold. She arched her spine when his middle finger brushed her womanhood. Her breathing became louder, her eyelids hooded. Her breasts strained against the dress.

Fargo removed his spurs, shucked his gunbelt, and climbed on the bed beside her. Marcy gripped him by the back of the neck, then locked her mouth to his in a long, hot, passionate kiss. He could feel himself growing rock-hard. His left hand swooped to her breasts and massaged them both, gently tweaking the nipples, which were as hard as he was. She pushed her hips against him, eager to get to the main course.

Fargo took his sweet time. He tweaked her glorious mounds and caressed her willowy legs until she was panting like someone who had just run a mile. Her long nails raked his shoulders, his arms, his back, bringing him to a fever pitch of raw desire.

When the time came to undress her, Fargo went about it slowly. He kissed every inch of exposed skin, he nuzzled her throat, he nibbled on her earlobes. Her nipples were so sensitive that when he lowered his mouth to one and swirled it with his tongue, she cried out softly and clung to him as if she would never let him go.

Soon Marcy tugged at his shirt. As Fargo drew back to strip it off, her hand dived under his pants. The soft sensation of her palm wrapping around his pole almost made him rush things. He steeled himself as she stroked him, refusing to explode until the right moment came along.

"You're so big!" the brunette breathed. "I had no idea."

Fargo could not get enough of her pillowy globes. They were as ripe as melons, as creamy as milk. He lathered and kissed them until they were slick all over. Gripping the bottom of each, he squeezed just hard enough to induce Marcy to toss back her head and gasp.

"Oooooohhhhhh!" Marcy groaned. "You sure know how to stoke a girl's fire!"

"I aim to please," Fargo joked. He kissed his way lower, to her navel, then to the thick thatch below. The dank scent of her tunnel was enough to make his mouth water all over again. When he clamped it to her nether lips, Marcy bucked like a mustang. It was all he could do to hold on. She wheezed. She plunged. She bounced the bed to where it seemed about to fall apart.

Fargo delved deep into her, feeding the fire he had kindled. Her thighs closed on his head, pinning him in place. As if that were not enough, her hands entwined with his hair so he couldn't pull away even if he wanted to. He flicked and licked until his tongue was sore, yet still she wasn't satisfied.

At last Fargo pried loose. Pushing onto his knees, he lowered himself on top of her. She tried to enclose him in her velvet sheath but he held off to heighten their mutual suspense. His hands roamed her lush figure from head to knee, kneading flesh softer than her pillow.

"Yeeeesssss!" Marcy whispered. "I'm ready any time you are!"

Fargo didn't doubt it for a minute, but he still delayed. Her nipples received more attention. He probed her crack, then slid in a middle finger. She reacted by trying to heave both of them at the ceiling. At his first stroke, she nearly went berserk with unbridled lust. Her lips were everywhere. Her hands flew over him. She was a volcano waiting to blow. All she needed was a little boost to send her over the brink.

Two fingers about drove her wild with abandon. She drew blood clawing his shoulders. She pulled on his hair so roughly, it hurt. She was a wildcat who just couldn't get enough of him. Her mouth covered his. Her tongue smothered his. She sucked as if striving to inhale his mouth into hers.

It had an effect. Fargo's organ throbbed for release. He

could no longer hold off. Positioning himself, he fed the tip of his manhood into her, and when she tensed in breathless anticipation, he slammed into her to the hilt, his battering ram penetrating her womanly fortress.

"Uhhhhhhhh!" was the only sound Marcy made. Clasping him close, she pumped her bottom faster than a road runner could run, slapping into him again and again and again.

Friction brought Fargo near the brink but he held the explosion back by sheer force of will. He met her ardor with equal fire, matching her tit for tat. They began to rock as one, in rhythm with one another. Soft cries that meant nothing issued from her cherry red lips. Her legs wrapped around his waist and would not let go.

A tingling sensation formed at the base of Fargo's spine. Knowing what it meant, he stroked faster, wanting to bring her to the summit first. She obliged him by abruptly thrashing and moaning and flinging her head from side to side, her eyelids fluttering as if she were having a fit.

Fargo managed to stave off his own release until she started to quiet down. Then he let her have it, driving into her with twice as much vigor. The tingling built until it could no longer be contained. He erupted with the force of a keg of black powder, his body and hers molded together as if they were a single piece of sculpture.

"Oh, yeeeessssssss!" was torn from Marcy. She heaved up off the mattress.

The hammering of the bed's legs drowned out whatever else she said. Fargo kept plunging into her for as long as he could. Finally, exhausted, he coasted to a stop and slumped onto her breasts. She held him fast, her lips pressed to his neck, her hot breath fanning his ear.

Fargo dozed. How much longer it was that he rolled off her, he couldn't say. All he knew for sure was that in the chill early hours of the morning she woke up and covered them both with blankets before snuggling at his side. Again he drifted off, to be awakened hours later by a golden shaft of sunlight entering the sole window and striking him in the face. He squinted against the glare, then rose on an elbow.

Marcy still slumbered. She wore a smile, and every so often she would mutter in her sleep words too faint to hear.

Sliding off the bed without waking her, Fargo dressed and strapped on his gunbelt. The good night's rest had invigorated him. He decided to let her sleep while he stretched his legs and got some fresh air. Not bothering with his hat, he quietly crept out and closed the door behind him.

Nearby, the Ovaro cropped grass. As Fargo moved toward the stallion, it lifted its head and looked at him, its ears pricked. Fargo took another couple of steps before realizing that the pinto was staring *past* him, not at him, and he started to twist to learn why.

That was when a cold command rang out. "Don't twitch another muscle, mister, or we'll drop you where you stand!"

3

Skye Fargo did as the speaker commanded. Something—a sixth sense honed by years of surviving in the wilds—told him that the man wasn't bluffing; that if he made a stab for his Colt, he'd be dead before he cleared leather. Ever so slowly, he looked up.

Eight men ringed him, seven of them with either a leveled rifle or a drawn pistol. They had hard faces, harder eyes. They were men who would kill their own mothers if there was money to be made in doing it, then go out and down a few drinks in her memory.

Fargo pursed his lips, annoyed at himself. He should not have been so careless. It was obvious they had been lying in wait for him, and had just risen from concealment. Two of the eight he recognized: Bob Hackett and Fess Webster, the latter with his wrist crudely bandaged. A third man Fargo also knew, even though they had never met before. There was only one person it could be.

Wolf Rollins was as tall as Fargo but even more powerfully built, with wide, flaring shoulders and a narrow waist adorned by a pair of ivory-handled Colts. His features resembled those of the animal he was named after. Bushy brows crowned dark, volcanic eyes. His nose was long and tapered; his mouth, downright cruel. When the man smiled, as he did now, he looked so wolfish it was uncanny. He wore a gray shirt, black pants, and a wide-brimmed black hat.

"You know who I am, don't you?"

Fargo nodded. There was no sense in denying it. But he was troubled. It almost seemed as if the man had read his thoughts.

Wolf Rollins advanced, his body rippling with raw force. The man had a certain presence, as if he radiated vitality, like the sun. Only his vitality had nothing to do with light and life. His was a chilling presence, an almost physical evil that somehow made itself known to those around him.

Only once or twice before had Fargo met anyone like this man. He held himself still as Rollins halted and scrutinized him from head to boots. The others also closed in, but they stayed far enough back to have clear shots if he tried anything.

"You have a handle?" their leader asked.

Fargo told him. Up close, he could see what appeared to be tiny specks of silver dancing in Rollins's dark eyes. He dismissed them as a trick of the morning sun.

"Fargo?" Wolf Rollins repeated. "Why does that name sound familiar to me? We've never met."

Fess Webster picked that moment to step forward and gesture with the six-shooter he held. "Why are you jawing with this bastard, boss? I say we kill him right here and now for what he did to Jenkins and me!"

If Fargo had blinked, he would have missed what happened next. Wolf Rollins spun and swung, human lightning unleashed, backhanding Fess Webster across the face. It was no more than a tap, yet such was Rollins's strength that the underling was knocked onto his backside and sat there dumbfounded, his cheek stung livid red.

Wolf loomed over the cutthroat, who made no attempt to use the revolver he held. "Did my ears deceive me? Did I hear what I think I heard?" Bending, Wolf Rollins gripped the front of Webster's shirt. Slowly, almost gently, Webster was lifted several inches off the ground. "*You* say we should kill him? When did we start doing what you want, Fess, and not what *I* want?"

Fess Webster was noticeably terrified. Lower lip quivering, he blurted, "Never, Wolf! I didn't mean it to come out the way it did! I'd never buck you! You know that!" Webster gulped, sweat breaking out all over his face. "It's just that he cut me, is all. I got so mad there for a second, I wasn't thinking straight."

Wolf glanced at the bandage, then released the gunman's

shirt and smoothed it. "Congratulations, Fess. I accept your excuse. But don't ever let it happen again. The next time, I might not be so forgiving."

Webster exhaled so loud, they all heard him.

Almost without exerting himself, Wolf Rollins hoisted the man to his feet. "Now be quiet while I have my say, will you? You know how I hate to be interrupted."

To say Fargo was amazed would be an understatement. Wolf Rollins was not at all as he had expected the man to be. Most bad men were more like Webster—grungy, vicious vermin who would pump lead into someone without giving it a second thought. Anyone who crossed them, anyone they took a dislike to, was as good as dead. Few were very smart.

Rollins was an exception. Not only was the man as strong as an ox, he had rare intelligence for someone who made his living by the gun. It showed in the way he talked, the way he acted, in the set of his features, even in the clean clothes he wore. Rollins was as different from Webster and the rest of Webster's breed as night was from day. Yet, deep down, they shared one similar trait. They were natural-born killers.

Suddenly, at a gesture from their leader, several of the gang surrounded Fargo. His arms were seized. Wolf Rollins plucked the Colt from its holster, admired the pistol a few moments, then tossed it down near the shack.

"You won't be needing that anymore."

Crouching, Wolf ran his hand over both of Fargo's boots. He chuckled as he pulled out the Arkansas toothpick and wagged it at Fess Webster. "This little thing is what he cut you with? To hear you squawk last night, it had to be a sword."

Several men laughed. If Webster resented being poked fun at, he wisely held his tongue.

Wolf Rollins stood. Tapping the toothpick against his other hand, he said, "No one kills one of my men and lives to tell of it." He pressed the tip of the blade against Fargo's jaw. "It's nothing personal, you understand. I just have a certain reputation to uphold."

It was then that the door to the shack opened. Hope

flared in Fargo at the sight of Marcy dressed in a heavy robe, his Henry in her hands. All she had to do was cover Rollins long enough for him to reclaim the Colt.

"As I live and breathe," Wolf declared, and took a step back as if in shock. "Here I thought you never rolled out of the sack before noon."

Marcy looked at him. She smiled. "Morning, lover."

Fargo felt a sinking sensation in his gut as Wolf went over, embraced her, and gave her a kiss that lingered on and on. None of the others acted the least bit surprised. A couple of them snickered. When Wolf broke the hug, he beamed.

"Thanks for keeping this hombre around until I could get here."

The brunette rubbed against Rollins and said huskily, "My pleasure." Her laugh was as brittle as dry wood. "The idiot is probably the only one in these parts who doesn't know that I'm your girl."

They all thought that hilarious.

Fargo had been played the fool before, but this time rankled more than most. He was furious, yet there was nothing he could do. Not being held as he was. Not with so many guns trained on him.

Wolf turned. "There's one thing I need to know before we get down to business, mister. Why did you kill Art Jenkins? What did he ever do to you?"

Marcy responded before Fargo could. "I know. I overheard him talking to Sullivan." She repeated, practically word for word, everything Fargo had told the Irishman.

A scowl lent Rollins a sadistic aspect. "If Jenkins were still alive, I'd kill him myself. The damn jackass! So what if a few questions were asked about McDermott? I never told him to go around busting heads!" Rollins held the toothpick as if eager to bury it in someone. "Art was supposed to keep his ears open and report anything of interest back to me. That was all." He glanced at Skye. "It must rile you, knowing you're about to die because one of my men couldn't follow orders."

Fargo didn't say a word. He was girding himself to make a bid for his life. Despite the odds, he was not going to go out without a fight. Gauging the distance to his Colt, to Marcy, and to the shack door, he glanced at the men holding him. The one on the left had not set himself and would be easy to throw off balance.

Wolf Rollins and Marcy were talking in low tones. A few of the hardcases had relaxed and let the muzzles of their hardware droop. There would never be a better time.

Exploding into action, Fargo whipped the man on the left into the man on the right and they both went down, entangled in a knot. Yelps and shouts broke out as he dived for the Colt, his right arm outstretched. His fingers were about to curl around the butt when a brutal blow caught him low on the chest. Lancing pain racked him as he was flung to one side. His hand scraped grass and came up empty. Surging onto his knees, Fargo was dimly aware of a tall figure near him, of a boot being cocked for another kick.

Fargo threw up an arm to block the kick, and the next moment he was struck from behind, a jolting smash that flattened him and left his head spinning. He tried to rise but his wrists were clamped in iron holds and a knee gouged into his spine. Someone laughed.

"Lift him," Wolf Rollins said.

Hardcases hemmed Fargo in. By the shack, Marcy was grinning. He would have loved to wipe it off her face but he had a more urgent matter to attend to, namely staying alive. Rollins stepped in front of him.

"Nice try, mister. You've got grit, I'll give you that."

Fargo kneed him. Or attempted to. Somehow Wolf skipped aside, then shifted and slammed a fist into Fargo's abdomen. Fargo had been punched before, but seldom like this, seldom so hard that it felt as if all his internal organs had been pulped. His breath whooshed from his lungs. He would have fallen if not for the men holding him.

"Yes, sir," Wolf Rollins said, and there was no sarcasm in his tone. "Gritty as fish eggs rolled in sand."

It was a high compliment but Fargo was in no frame of mind to appreciate it. He saw a foot next to his and stomped the toes for all he was worth. A gunman howled. Someone else roared with mirth. Another fist to the stomach made the world blink out and for several seconds he was barely conscious. Dimly, he heard Rollins.

"Have fun, boys. But don't kill him yet. We'll save that for later."

Fargo was released. He hit the ground seconds before fists and feet commenced hitting him, pounding his back and shoulders and chest. Weak as a kitten, he attempted to protect himself but it was hopeless. The agony was beyond belief, agony to end all agony, and after a while he gratefully grew numb to it. He collapsed. Only then did the beating stopped.

The sky was a blur. A face materialized above him. Wolf Rollins stared at him, puzzled. "What the hell are you made of, mister? You never let out a peep."

Marshalling the last of his strength, Fargo swung. He intended to bash Rollins on the jaw but he was much too slow. His arm was caught, was trapped under the killer's elbow.

"Damn! Don't you ever give up?"

Marcy called out. "Kill him, lover! Kill him now! A man like that is too dangerous to treat lightly!"

Wolf's reply was like the crack of a bullwhip. "Not you too? Doesn't anyone pay attention to anything I say? No one tells me what to do! I'll make wolf meat of him when I'm ready, and not before."

"It's your funeral," the brunette said.

Rollins disappeared from above Fargo. A loud smack rang out. Marcy said something and was slapped again. Fargo didn't feel the least bit sorry for her. He used the respite to collect his wits and prepare himself to make one last try as soon as Wolf came back. But before that could happen, a pair of husky killers grabbed him by the arms and jackknifed him to his feet, none too gently.

Wolf stood over Marcy, who cowered against the door jamb with a hand pressed to her face. "Are there any other comments you'd like to make, whore?"

Marcy shook her head vigorously.

"Good!" Rotating on a heel, Wolf Rollins stepped toward Fargo. He still held the toothpick, which he wagged in a small circle. "Maybe she has a point, though. You're about the toughest thing on two legs I've ever come across. It makes sense to slit your throat while I can."

Unable to break free, Fargo worked his mouth to spit in his tormentor's smug face. But his mouth was too dry. The best he could do was rasp, "Go to hell!"

"You first, I reckon," Wolf said. His arm was flung wide for the fatal flash. Those unusual eyes of his were alive with glee. Then they changed. They drifted past Fargo and narrowed. Resentment replaced the glee. "What the hell do you want?"

"No more," someone said. It was a voice that Fargo was sure he had heard before, but he couldn't quite place it.

"Don't poke your nose where it doesn't belong," Wolf Rollins snapped.

"I can't let you do it," the newcomer stated. "Not here, not in the middle of town."

Wolf Rollins lowered his arm. "What are you talking about? This flea-ridden dump isn't even on any map yet. It'll be years before it officially becomes a town, if ever." He snorted. "You jackasses can't even decide on a name."

"Be that as it may," the newcomer said, "I can't stand by and let you murder people right out in broad daylight. What you do off in the wilds is your affair. But this . . ."

The accent nudged Fargo's pain-racked memory. It was the Irishman. But why would Sullivan buck a man like Rollins on his account? He hardly knew the man.

Wolf Rollins was thinking along similar lines. Casting the toothpick down, he jabbed a thumb at Fargo. "Why stick your neck out for him? What am I missing here?"

Sullivan sighed. "I doubt that I could explain it to your satisfaction. Suffice it to say that there is a line I won't cross, and a line I can't let you cross. Not here. Not right out back of my establishment."

"You're jabbering nonsense," Wolf declared. For a few seconds his hands were poised above his twin ivory-handled revolvers. Then he motioned in disgust and walked off. "One of these times you'll prod me too far, Irishman. And when that happens, no brother in high places is going to save you. Remember that."

The rabid wolves who ran with Rollins appeared to be as astounded as Fargo.

Wolf stalked toward the corner of the saloon. "You get your way this time, Sullivan. But he had better not be here when I'm done with my whiskey."

Hackett, Webster, and the rest reluctantly drifted after him, Webster looking back and fingering his pistol. They were gone in no time.

Marcy entered her shack, the door slamming behind her.

Fargo, bewildered, was left standing there. He tried to take a step and swayed. Another step, and his legs turned to mush. Wildly, he flailed for support that wasn't there. As he toppled, an arm hooked his chest, righting him.

"Take it easy," Sullivan said. "A man in your condition shouldn't do much moving around."

It hurt to talk but Fargo did so anyway. "You heard your friend. I have to light a shuck while I can."

"Wolf Rollins is hardly my friend," Sullivan said, but he did not elaborate.

Fargo saw the toothpick. Straightening, he locked his knees and shuffled to it. When he began to bend down, dizziness swamped him. The grass spun. The knife blurred. He dipped to one knee and closed his eyes until the sickening sensation passed.

The knife went into its sheath. Next Fargo claimed the Colt, brushing dirt off the barrel. It surprised him that Rollins had left it there, but even more surprising was the Henry, lying close to the shack. He used it for a crutch, resting while he caught his breath, Sullivan watching him the whole time. "Something on your mind?" he demanded.

"What keeps you going? Most men would have keeled over long ago."

An answer was on the tip of Fargo's tongue, but at that juncture the shack door opened. Marcy came out, bearing his saddle. Grunting, she plopped it down, went back in, and came out in a few moments carrying his saddle blanket, bedroll, hat and saddlebags, which she added to the pile.

"I believe these are yours, handsome," she said with no malice. "Pity about how things turned out. But you never should have crossed Wolf. He's top dog in these parts." She paused in the doorway. "One of these days he's going to take me to California. He gave me his word."

Fargo couldn't help himself. "And you're stupid enough to believe him?"

The door slammed once more, louder than the first time.

It took every last bit of energy Fargo had left but he made it to the pile and carried the blanket to the Ovaro. He had to lean on the pinto a while before he could spread the blanket out. Stepping back, he nearly bumped into the Irishman, who held his saddle.

"Out of the way, if you don't mind."

Fargo was in no shape to object. He let Sullivan saddle up, let the other man tie on his bedroll and saddlebags. "I owe you," he said when the stallion was ready to go.

"Like hell. I only did what was right."

So many questions needed to be asked. Fargo opened his mouth to do so, then tensed as harsh voices approached from the front of the saloon.

"It must be Wolf and his boys!" Sullivan said, holding out Fargo's hat. "Get going while you can! I doubt that I can talk him out of taking your life a second time."

No incentive was needed. Grasping the horn, Fargo lifted his right boot and slid it into the stirrup. But when he attempted to pull himself onto the hurricane deck, his traitorous arms refused to obey. If not for Sullivan giving him a hasty boost, he never would have managed it. Wheeling the Ovaro, he touched his hat brim and was off, trotting eastward past a short row of tents and buildings. As he came to the edge of the forest, shouts rang out. So did a shot.

Fargo applied his spurs. Lead chipped nearby branches as he sped into the pines. Cutting to the left, he put a cluster of large boulders between him and the shooters. Bits of stone chipped by zinging slugs flew so close to his ear that he heard them whiz by. Then he was out of range and bending low to ride like the wind.

There was only one problem. The fierce beating had taken more out of Fargo than he had been willing to admit. Now, put to the test, to his dismay, he found that his sinews were still as weak as those of a day old kitten's.

To add humiliation to the hurt, Fargo was forced to pull

leather, to grab onto the apple for dear life. It was a supreme insult to any horseman worthy of the name, but it was all he could do to stay in the saddle.

An incline brought Fargo to the crest of a low ridge overlooking Pagosa Springs. Mounted men were racing eastward down the dusty street, whooping and hollering. They were too far off to identify but he could guess who they were.

Wolf Rollins and company aimed to have some sport at his expense.

Cutting the reins, Fargo rode higher. His only hope, as he saw it, was to get over the Divide before they caught up with him. To do that, he had to reach Wolf Creek Pass well ahead of the human wolf pack thirsting for his blood.

Wolf Creek Pass. One of the highest in the Rockies, at an elevation of over ten thousand feet, it was passable only three seasons out of four. In winter snow piled to monstrous depths, and many an unwary greenhorn had perished trying to get through. Even during warmer months it was perilous, with a series of steep switchbacks leading from a verdant valley floor to the stark summit.

It would take all the skill Fargo had to get there before he was overtaken, and once there, to get over the top without an accident. He knuckled down to the task of riding, weaving among the tall firs and past stands of slender aspens shimmering in the brisk mountain breeze.

Soon Fargo came to the San Juan River. Crossing, he rode parallel to it, bearing to the northwest, sticking to the beaten path to make better time. His battered, bruised body protested every lope of his mount. He broke out in a cold sweat and had to shake himself again and again to ward off gnawing weakness. It became hard to think so he stopped trying.

Presently, Fargo came to where the San Juan forked. Without slowing he took the right-hand branch and rode on, lashing the stallion with the reins. It was quite a while before he realized that something was wrong. Slowing, he looked around, seeking landmarks.

Fargo had been over Wolf Creek Pass before. He knew that to reach it from the west, a rider had to take the West

Fork of the San Juan River. In his sluggish state, he had erred. He had taken the East Fork, which would bring him nowhere near the pass.

Mad at himself for having made such a harebrained blunder, Fargo reined to the left to go back the way he had come. As always, the Ovaro instantly responded, but for once it would have been better if the stallion had balked. Because in his haste, Fargo failed to take into account the narrow trail he was on. He saw a low limb blossom before his eyes as if by magic and he hauled on the reins, a fraction too late.

The previous pain was nothing compared to this. Fargo's skull seemed to rupture like a ripe melon. The last sight he saw was the earth rushing up to meet him.

4

The acrid scent of smoke was the first clue Skye Fargo had that he was still alive. He opened his eyes, and promptly wished he hadn't.

Close to him a low fire crackled. The flames were not all that bright, yet when Fargo glanced at them, searing anguish ripped through his skull, anguish so great that he clenched his teeth and involuntarily groaned.

The rustle of someone moving alerted Fargo to the fact he wasn't alone. He jumped to the conclusion that Wolf Rollins had caught him, and that the outlaw was keeping him alive to kill later in some gruesome fashion. Automatically, his hand dropped to his Colt. But it wasn't there.

Fargo propped an elbow under him and attempted to rise. Suddenly his surroundings whirled as if in the grip of a tornado. Nausea assailed him. So weak he could hardly keep his eyes open, he fell back. And passed out.

It must have been hours later that Fargo woke up again. This time, in addition to the smoke, he was aware of another sensation, of a strange weight on his chest. It was not all that heavy, and whatever it was did not feel all that big. Carefully cracking his eyelids to avoid repeating his earlier mistake, he was flabbergasted to discover the Colt resting on his sternum. He wondered who would have put it there, and why? It was highly unlikely that any of the hardcases had taken pity on him.

Moving his right arm slowly so as not to draw attention to himself if others were watching, Fargo inched his fingers toward the Colt. Once they curled around the polished butt, he felt a smidgen better. At least now he could take a few of the bastards with him when he cashed in his chips.

Or could he? Fargo would not put it past Rollins or one of the other killers to have removed all the cartridges and then placed the revolver there to inspire false hope. In their warped way of thinking, it would be hilarious to have him sit up and blaze away with an empty cylinder.

Even so, Fargo could not just lie there. As the old saw went, it didn't do to look a gift horse in the mouth. He had to fight back. Curling back the hammer, he stiffened when it clicked, expecting an outcry. To his relief, there was none.

Fargo would have liked to lie there for an hour, resting. He was still much too weak, so weak he might not be able to stand. But there was only one way to find out. Bunching his stomach muscles, he hurled up into a sitting posture and swung the Colt toward the first figure he glimpsed. He almost snapped off a shot. Fortunately, the figure's long raven tresses froze him in confused shock.

It was a woman. An *Indian* woman, on her knees by the fire, mending a torn buckskin dress much like the beaded one she had on. She glanced up sharply. Her beautiful face betrayed no fear when she saw the cocked pistol. Instead, she smiled and said in a voice as rich as wild honey, "Would you shoot the person who saved your life, white man?"

Her English was thickly accented in a way that lent it a sultry appeal. Fargo, stupefied, could not get his mind to work as it should. All he could do was gawk.

"Why do you not speak, white man?" the woman asked. "Did the blow to your head deaden your brain?"

Embarrassed, Fargo lowered the Colt and eased down the hammer. He licked his lips before saying, "I'm sorry for pointing my gun at you. I thought you were someone else."

"The evil ones who were hunting you will never find you here. You need not worry. You are safe." She resumed stitching the supple buckskin, her deft fingers inserting a needle made of bone.

Still feeling partially dazed, Fargo looked around. He was in a structure very much like a tepee, yet considerably smaller. A score of long poles had been arranged in a conical shape and then covered by two or three elk hides. A small opening at the top permitted the smoke to waft up and out. He had seen such temporary shelters before. They were frequently used by a certain tribe. A closer look at the woman, at the style of her clothes and her hair, compelled him to say, "You are Ute."

The woman looked up. "You have had dealings with my people, white man?"

"My name is Fargo."

She said it a few times, rolling the two syllables on the tip of her pink tongue as if tasting them. "An unusual name. In your language, I would be called Morning Flower."

"How is it that you speak my tongue so well?" Fargo inquired, since few Utes ever went to the trouble of learning English. The reason was simple. The Utes despised all whites and anything that had to do with them. Fargo couldn't blame them, either.

Each year more and more whites planted roots in Ute territory, taking land the Utes had claimed for generations, eating game the Utes saw as their own. So far, widespread bloodshed had been avoided, but it was only a matter of time, in Fargo's opinion, before the whites would push the Utes to the breaking point.

The Utes were a proud people. Although they lived deep in the mountains, they had adopted many of the customs of the Plains tribes. They lived in tepees. They relied on the horse. They hunted buffalo regularly. While not as warlike as the Blackfeet or Apaches, they were able fighters and could hold their own against any other tribe. They were also a close-knit people, roaming the Rockies in large bands. They traveled from valley to valley, moving on to the next as game became scarce.

The shelter in which Fargo found himself was typical of those used by Ute hunting parties, who often roamed far and wide from their village. It led him to the conclusion that a roving group of hunters had found him and for reasons only they knew had decided to save his hide.

"Where is your man?" Fargo asked when she did not answer his first question.

Morning Flower's features clouded. "I do not have one."

Fargo didn't know what to make of that. Indians generally married their women off young. Among some tribes, as soon as a girl had her first menses she was eligible for courtship. A few tribes went so far as to have a crier go around the camp announcing the good news.

The Ute woman was in her twenties. She should have married long ago. Fargo guessed that she had lost her husband recently and not yet taken a new one. But then, if she were unattached, she would not be with a hunting party. It would be improper. "I'd like to speak to the warrior in charge," he said.

She paused in the act of inserting her needle. "In charge?" she repeated quizzically.

"The head of the hunting party you are with," Fargo clarified.

"There are no men here."

Fargo thought he understood. "They are all off hunting? How soon will they be back? I would like to learn what they intend to do with me."

The Ute woman stared into the crackling flames. "You are free to do as you want, white man. I am alone. There is no one else here but us."

"How can that be?" Fargo asked. It was unthinkable for the Utes to leave one of their women alone with a white.

"I found you, Fargo," Morning Flower said rather sadly. "I brought you to my camp two suns ago. I have looked after you ever since."

It was hard to say which revelation startled Fargo the most, the fact that she truly was all by herself or that he had been unconscious for over two days. His confusion must have shown, because she glanced at him and went on.

"I no longer live with my people. Most of them want nothing to do with me. I am, as you would say, an outcast."

Fargo had heard of Indians casting members out, but it was rarely done. Only the most vile of acts merited being banished. Murder of a fellow tribal member was one, rape another. He wanted to press her for details, but it went against his grain to pry into someone else's personal affairs. So all he said was, "I'm sorry to hear it."

Morning Flower sighed. "I brought it on myself. I grew fond of a white man, a trapper who traded with my people from time to time. He was very handsome, my Joe Sirak. My heart and his heart became one."

So that was it, Fargo mused. She had fallen in love with a white man and been booted from her band. "It's a shame your people wouldn't let the two of you live with them."

"Oh, we did, for five winters," Morning Flower said. "They were the happiest days of my life. Joe taught me your tongue. I taught him ours. We tried hard to have little ones, but I never grew heavy with child."

Fargo couldn't help himself. "What happened to him?"

The woman saddened more than ever. "A warrior named Stalking Wolf decided that he wanted me. He told me to leave Joe and go live with him. I refused, and he attacked my Joe." Her voice dropped. "Joe killed him. And even though Stalking Wolf was to blame, his brother, Tall Bear, called a council and convinced the elders to banish Joe and me."

"Then were is Sirak now?"

It was a while before the pretty Ute answered. "Rubbed out. One day he did not come back from checking his trap line, so I went looking for him. He had been shot in the back with an arrow. I think Tall Bear did it." Absently, she poked at the fire with a stick. "I buried Joe and went back to our lodge, only to find it had been burned to the ground while I was gone. I saved what I could and went off to be by myself. For over three moons now I have lived alone."

"Tall Bear has not bothered you since?"

Morning Flower frowned and jabbed the stick hard. "I move around a lot, but he has still tracked me down two times to demand that I go back and live with him. He says it is the only way his brother's spirit will be at peace. Each time I have refused. Each time he has grown madder. I would not be surprised if he kills me one day. He is a mad wolf, that one."

Fargo felt extremely sorry for her. They were a lot alike, she and him. Morning Flower had no way of knowing that once he had lived with the Sioux and been very much in love with a Sioux maiden, only to have her die in his arms, a victim of the rampant hatred between whites and the red man. And they had both made enemies of cold-blooded killers who would not rest until they were held to account.

To change the subject, Fargo said, "I want to thank you for all you've done for me. If there is ever anything I can do to repay the favor, all you have to do is ask."

"You owe me nothing," Morning Flower said. "I did what I did because you were someone in need of help." She managed a wan smile. "And you also look a lot like my Joe."

An awkward silence descended. Fargo could not help but note how lush her figure was, how beautiful she looked with the firelight playing over her smooth face. She reminded him so much of the Sioux maiden who had once meant so much to him that his innards twisted into a knot and he choked back a constriction in his throat. Long ago he had put up a wall deep in his mind, a barrier to keep him from ever thinking about her.

"You must be hungry, Fargo," Morning Flower said. "I forced you to drink and eat a little since I first brought you here, but you would not take much."

The mention of food made Fargo realize how ravenous he really was. "I could eat a horse," he said.

Morning Flower grinned. "Since I doubt you want to eat yours, and I will not let you eat mine, we must make do with the stew I prepared this morning." Turning, she brought a small pot into view and placed it on a metal tripod over the fire. "As soon as it is hot enough, we will eat."

Fargo leaned on an elbow. He had not realized that he was still holding the Colt, and he quickly slid it into his holster. Over by the entrance flap his belongings were piled. The Henry leaned against a pole, as did a Sharps Model 1852 carbine with a slanting breech that must have belonged to the trapper, Joe Sirak.

Fargo thought of a question he should pose. "You mentioned the evil ones who are hunting me. Where did you see them?"

"They came up the east branch of the river soon after I found you. If I had not dragged you into the brush and hid your horse, you would not be alive." Morning Flower produced a wooden ladle and began stirring the stew. "I watched them. They hunted for your tracks but I had erased them too well."

"Then I owe you my life twice over," Fargo said.

Morning Flower shrugged. "Wolf and his men are killers, not trackers. I would not have fooled one of my own people."

"You know Wolf Rollins?"

"He and his butchers have killed some of our people. Shot them down, with no chance to defend themselves. And his men laughed as they did it." Morning Flower raised the ladle to her lips. "Our warriors have marked him for death, but he is sly, that one. They have yet to catch him off guard."

Fargo could only hope that the Utes didn't ambush Rollins before he recuperated enough to go after the man himself. He had a score to settle, and he didn't want to be denied the satisfaction of paying the man back.

"Wolf and his men gave up after a while. They rode west," Morning Flower revealed. "Tall Bear has told me that they have a secret camp in a gorge two days' ride from here."

The information was worth remembering. For the moment, though, all Fargo could think of was how famished he happened to be, and the bubbling broth at the top of the pot.

Outside, a horse nickered. Fargo recognized the Ovaro. Another animal whinnied. Then hooves drummed the earth. The Ute woman dropped the ladle and spun.

"It has to be Tall Bear! No one else ever pays me a visit." Morning Flower moved to the entrance and grabbed the Sharps carbine. "He must not learn you are here!"

Fargo was going to caution her that it might not be the Ute warrior, that Wolf Rollins might have come back and found them after all, but she pushed the flap wide and was gone before he could say a word. Painfully shoving himself to his hands and knees, he scurried to the Henry.

A deep voice barked, and it wasn't in English. Quietly levering a round into the rifle's chamber, Fargo bellied to the flap. Using a forefinger, he cracked the bottom edge and put an eye to the opening. The angle was such that he had to twist his head to see clearly.

Morning Flower had planted herself a stride from the opening, the Sharps cradled in her left arm. She faced three mounted warriors, foremost among them a lanky man in a heavily fringed buckskin shirt and leggings. That would be Tall Bear, Fargo deduced. All three were armed with broad bows, quivers full of arrows, and big knives.

Fargo did not know the Ute tongue but he did his best to follow the drift of their talk. It soon became clear that Morning Flower's comments were not to Tall Bear's liking. The warrior grew more and more angry, gesturing severely at her and at her small makeshift lodge.

Soon one of the other Utes pointed at the Ovaro and made a remark. Tall Bear seemed to take note of the stallion for the first time. Clearly troubled, he interrogated the woman, whose answers appeared to satisfy him.

In due course Tall Bear grunted and motioned. The three men turned their mounts and rode off in single file, disappearing in dense pines.

Morning Flower did not move until a long time after they were gone. As she bent to enter, Fargo moved back out of the way. She glanced at the Henry, then leaned the Sharps in the same spot it had been before her unwanted guests arrived.

"You need rest badly. You should have laid down. I would not have let them harm you."

Fargo set his rifle in front of him as he stretched out on his side. "It wasn't me I was worried about."

About to sit, Morning Flower gave him a curious stare. "Why do you care what happens to me?"

"You helped me when I needed it most, didn't you?" Fargo countered, at a loss to understand why she was making such a fuss. She should be grateful, not upset. "What were the two of you talking about?"

"The usual," Morning Flower said. "He demanded that I stop living alone and move into his lodge. I told him that I am happy the way things are, and I do not plan to change my ways." She took up her post by the pot. "He also asked about your horse. I told him that it belonged to a white man."

"He didn't ask where the white man was?"

The Ute woman chuckled. "Somehow I gave him the idea I had stolen it from one of Wolf's men," she said with mock innocence. "He wanted your pinto for himself but I refused to let him have it. If I am lucky, he will not pay me another visit for many moons."

Fargo was impressed. Few women in any tribe would dare to talk back to a prominent warrior. She had shown a lot of spunk. Evidently she had an independent streak almost as wide as his.

In a few minutes the stew was done to Morning Flower's satisfaction. She filled a bark bowl to the brim and passed it to him, along with an old, battered spoon. Fargo ate with relish, much too fast, despite a warning from her to slow down. He gobbled a second bowl, started in on a third, and that was when it caught up with him. About to shovel more into his mouth, he nearly bent in half as a cramp seared his gut.

Morning Flower shook her head. "Why are all men so stubborn? White or Indian, it does not matter. A woman can talk until her lips fall off, and still men do not listen."

Fargo grinned despite the pain. "It would be a shame to lose a fine pair of lips like yours. Next time, I'll heed your advice." Another cramp sawed his insides. He put down the bowl before he spilled it.

"That is another thing about men," Morning Flower said. "They love to make promises women know they can never keep. Why is that?"

Fargo put a hand on his stomach, wishing the spasms would subside. "I'll answer that one if you can tell me why women always think they know all there is to know about a man, even if the two have barely met."

Morning Flower had lovely teeth. "All women know the answer to that one. Men are like children. They wear their emotions on their faces. It is easy to know what they will do before they do it."

Laughing, Fargo quit while he was behind. If there was one thing he had learned, it was to never argue with women. Most of them really believed they were smarter than any man who had ever lived. And those who didn't liked to pretend they were.

Lying on his back, Fargo bided time until the discomfort went away. It was his own fault for having gorged on an empty stomach, but he just couldn't help himself. Morning Flower made just about the tastiest stew he had ever eaten.

Later, flushed with new strength, Fargo went out for some fresh air. Twilight shrouded the Rockies. From the northwest gusted a welcome cool breeze. A flock of noisy sparrows were roosting in a tree close to the Ute woman's camp, situated in a clearing that bordered a bubbling creek so clear, he could see the tiniest pebbles on the bottom.

Morning Flower was busy giving her mare a rubdown with a short porcupine quill brush. He walked over and sat on a log to watch. Fading rays of sunlight lent a golden luster to her natural beauty.

"Men never learn," she said without looking up.

"What did I do now?" Fargo asked. "All I wanted was to stretch my legs."

"And what will you want to do tomorrow? Go riding for a few hours? Or maybe run up and down a mountain for exercise?" Straightening, she gave him the sort of a look an angry mother might give a child who had misbehaved, and repeated herself. "Men never learn."

Fargo had always held to the view that only a complete jackass stepped into the same bear trap twice. So he brought up something else. Nodding at the high peak to the north of her camp, he said, "Isn't that Treasure Mountain?"

Morning Flower stopped stroking. "Why do you want to know?"

"There's a prospector somewhere up there by the name of McDermott. Wolf Rollins has been giving him a hard time."

The woman faced around. "What does that have to do with you? Are you a friend of McDermott's?"

"Never met the gent," Fargo confessed. "But the way I see it, any enemy of Rollins's is a friend of mine."

Coming closer, Morning Flower peered deep into his eyes as if trying to see into his very soul. "Is that all there is to it? Are you sure you do not have another reason for wanting to find McDermott."

"Such as?"

"Such as the silver he found. Even I know about the ore he showed everyone. They say he will be very rich one day." Her dark eyes held a hint of mistrust. "Some white men would do anything to get their hands on the shiny metal. They would lie, steal, even kill. My Joe told me it is a sickness that puts your brains in a whirl."

"Your Joe knew human nature," Fargo said. "But believe me, I don't mean McDermott any harm. All I want to do is offer the man my help if he wants it."

"Nothing else?"

"Nothing else."

Morning Flower nodded. "I believe you. Now all you must do is convince him."

"That shouldn't be too hard," Fargo said. No sooner were the words out of his mouth than the muzzle of a rifle barrel was thrust past his left temple and he heard a hammer being cocked.

"I like a yahoo with confidence," said whoever held the gun. "You'll need it, too. Because if you don't persuade me, sonny, I'm liable to blow your brains out!"

5

Skye Fargo's reflexes were second to none. Even in his weakened state, he could have thrown himself to one side, unlimbered the Colt, and fired twice before the man behind him spoke a single word. But he stayed seated and calm. His reason? Fargo knew that Morning Flower must have seen the stranger approach, yet she had displayed no alarm, nor did she make a dive for the Sharps propped at the far end of the log. That meant she knew the newcomer; he was someone she trusted. And that was good enough for Fargo.

Shifting, Fargo glanced around. From the sound of the stranger's voice, he assumed the man was about average height. But where there should be a head, there was empty air. Fargo dipped his gaze lower. Then lower still, to the crown of a battered floppy hat that had seen more years than he had lived. Under the hat was a great bushy head bristling with a salt-and-pepper beard, crowning a body that was all of four feet tall, if that.

"I'll be damned," Fargo said.

"Hardly, sir," said the undersized apparition. "I'm the one who was cursed with the heart of a lion in the body of a lamb! I'm the one who has had to bear the slings and arrows of outrageous fortune my whole life, and all because half of me was left inside my dear mother's womb!"

Fargo didn't know quite what to say. People of the man's stature were about as common on the frontier as hen's teeth. "*You're* Ike McDermott?"

The prospector cocked a lively green eye. "What? You were expecting maybe Samson and Goliath rolled into one?" McDermott snorted, then a rolling rumble issued from his barrel chest, a booming laugh that would have done justice to a man three times as big. "Don't let my size fool you, sonny! I've licked a bear with nothing but a knife in my hand, and I've never been beaten at arm wrestling."

Fargo believed him. The prospector had massive upper arms to match his powerful chest. "I've just never met a dwarf before," he remarked.

McDermott's good humor vanished in an instant. Gripping his rifle with both brawny hands, he shook it as if it were Fargo's throat. "Lord, how I hate that word! A dwarf, sonny, is someone of small statue, sure enough. But a dwarf's body is out of proportion." Standing tall, he thrust out his chest and snapped, "As you can plainly see, my build is just right for my size. In fact, it's perfect! Wouldn't you agree?"

It was, so Fargo did.

Appeased, McDermott came around the log to give Morning Flower a warm hug. She responded in kind, clearly delighted to see him. "Where did you find the stray, my dear?" the prospector asked in a mock low tone. "He's couth enough, I suppose, but a bit too tall for my tastes."

The two of them cackled. Sighing, Fargo rested an elbow on his knee and his chin in his hand. No one had ever called him "couth" before. He wondered what the hell it meant.

McDermott turned. "Just so you'll know, sir. There is a new word making the rounds to describe a person like me." He paused for effect. "Midget!"

"Midget?"

The prospector split a grin. "It has a certain ring to it, don't you think? Pleasing to the ear, but not distracting. Elegant, yet precise. Appropriate, yet not overstated." He said the word again, softly, lovingly, then asked, "What do you think?"

"Mister, I don't have any damn idea what you're babbling about," Fargo admitted. "To me, a word is just a word. As for your size, so what if you're not seven feet tall? You're a man, aren't you? Just like other men?"

Ike McDermott took a step back and placed a hand to his chest. "As I live and breathe! That's it in a nutshell! The bard put it best. A rose by any other name . . ." His voice trailed off and tears came to the corners of his eyes. "I salute you, sir, for standing head and shoulders above the common herd, and I'm proud to call you my friend!" He suddenly stopped, as if he had remembered something important. "Who *are* you, by the way?"

Fargo let out another sigh. First Wolf Rollins, a confirmed killer who acted and talked more like a graduate of one of those fancy finishing schools back East, and now Ike McDermott, a loco midget whose mouth could power a steam engine if someone could only figure out how to harness all that energy. Maybe it was something in the water at this altitude, Fargo mused.

Morning Flower made the introductions. When she got to the part about seeing the gang of cutthroats, her visitor went into a funk.

"Wolf Rollins again! That devil in human guise! That serpent in a mortal coil!" McDermott held his rifle aloft and railed at the heavens. "How much longer will he be inflicted on us? How much longer must we endure the barbs of his vile breed?"

Fargo leaned toward the Ute woman. "Is he always like this?"

"Only when he is awake," Morning Flower responded, and started to chuckle. It sputtered into a frozen frown as her eyes lifted toward the stream. For a few moments she went rigid, then she moved quickly toward the Sharps but stopped short at a bellowed outcry.

Standing, Fargo whirled. His hand was inches from the Colt but it might as well have been miles.

The three Ute warriors had returned. They had circled back, left their mounts concealed in the forest, and crept into the clearing with arrows notched to the sinew strings of their immensely powerful bows. Two of those shafts were pointed at Fargo, the third at Ike McDermott.

Tall Bear wore a mask of hatred. His lips twitched, and he appeared on the verge of loosing his arrow at Fargo. He bobbed his head at the Ovaro, then growled at Morning Flower. She answered angrily while moving toward him but halted when he motioned for her to do so. They argued back and forth, Tall Bear growing madder by the moment.

Fargo would have given anything to be able to understand their tongue. Ike McDermott was listening closely, as if he did, so Fargo whispered, "Do you know what they're saying?"

"I catch snatches here and there," the prospector whispered back. "But not all of it makes sense to me." He pointed at the pinto. "For one thing, Tall Bear is real upset about that animal. He suspected that she was lying about it, so he snuck on back to spy on her." McDermott listened a bit. "Now he's accusing her of taking a new husband. You. And he aims to stake you out and skin you alive."

"What will they do to you?"

"Little old me?" McDermott chortled. "Hell, sonny. The Utes won't harm a hair on my head. Why do you think they've let me prospect on their land for so long when they drive off most other whites?"

"I have no idea."

McDermott patted his chest. "It's my size, of all things. They've never seen anyone quite like me, and somehow or other they took to the notion that I have mighty medicine, that I'm under the protection of the Great Mystery or whatever it is they call the Almighty. So they let me go my way in peace."

"Lucky you," Fargo said dryly.

"Oh, I still have to be careful," McDermott said. "A few of them would like nothing better than to slit my throat, but they're afraid of riling the spirits." He winked and snickered. "Thank God for religion, eh?"

Fargo saw no humor in the situation. He had to act while he still could, but the trees were too far off to offer cover and the lodge entrance was almost as far. A few strides would bring him to the Ovaro, but he had to pull out the picket pin before he could swing on and gallop off, and by then an arrow would bring him down.

Suddenly the warriors advanced. One of them stopped a few feet away and sighted down his shaft at Fargo's heart. If Fargo moved, he would die.

Tall Bear lowered his bow. Brusquely brushing Morning Flower aside, he snatched Fargo's Colt and handed it to the third Ute. Making as if to turn toward the prospector, he unexpectedly spun and struck Fargo across the mouth.

The blow staggered Fargo, but he didn't go down. He would have sprung on his tormentor and beaten Tall Bear senseless if not for the other Ute holding the drawn bow.

At a command from Tall Bear, Ike McDermott was relieved of his weapons. McDermott protested, but it did him no good. His Sharps, a brace of pistols, and a butcher knife were placed next to Morning Flower's rifle. The widow and the prospector were then herded closer to the lodge and had to stand there helplessly while Tall Bear and his friends dealt with Fargo.

The Utes worked swiftly, roughly. Tall Bear and one other seized Fargo by the arms and hauled him to the middle of the clearing. Throwing him onto his back, they stripped off his shirt and boots. While two warriors covered him, Tall Bear went off into the woods and shortly came back bearing four short sections from busted limbs. Using a large flat rock, he pounded them into the ground, two above Fargo, two near Fargo's feet.

Ignoring Morning Flower's protests, Tall Bear entered her small lodge. He was not in there long. In his left hand was a coiled rope.

Fargo had observed all this with mounting unease. Once he was tied to the stakes, the Utes could do as they damn well pleased. He kept hoping the pair covering him would let down their guard, but they were like statues, the barbed points of their arrows fixed unswervingly on his rib cage. Then a shadow fell across him and he looked up to see the spiteful sneer of Tall Bear.

The tall Ute cut four equal lengths of rope. Moving around to the upper stakes, he sank to one knee and reached for Fargo's left wrist.

That was when Ike McDermott let out with a ripsnorting caterwaul uncannily like the scream of a mountain lion. Instinctively, the three Utes glanced toward him.

It was the only opening Fargo was going to get. Flinging himself to the left, he grabbed hold of Tall Bear's right forearm and yanked, pulling the Ute down on top of him. As he did, an arrow thudded into the earth so close to his back that a feather brushed his skin. The last Ute, though, held his fire, unwilling to let fly for fear of accidentally hitting Tall Bear. Which was just what Fargo wanted.

They grappled. Tall Bear had sheathed his knife and strove furiously to reach it while Fargo strove just as furiously to prevent him. Out of the corners of his eyes Fargo could see the other warriors prancing around them, seeking an opening.

One abruptly drew a knife and skipped in close to stab him in the back but Fargo rolled in the opposite direction, pulling Tall Bear with him. The lunging Ute nearly buried the blade in Tall Bear's back, jerking it away at the last moment.

It was only delaying the inevitable. Fargo couldn't hold the three of them off forever. Sooner or later a warrior would connect. He had to break free and get his hands on a gun.

To that end, Fargo flipped onto his back, tucking his knees to his chest and letting go of Tall Bear, who immediately went to stand. Fargo lashed out, catching Tall Bear full on the chest with both feet. It bowled the Ute over and he crashed into another warrior, the man still holding a bow. Both went down in a jumble of arms and legs.

Fargo scrambled into a crouch as the last Ute pounced, cleaving the knife at his throat. Gliding in under the man's swing, Fargo delivered an uppercut that tottered the warrior backward.

For a few heartbeats, Fargo was in the clear. Spinning, he bounded toward the log and the pile of weapons. Heavy breaths and an equally heavy tread told him that at least one of the Utes was right on his heels. He didn't bother to look back. It didn't matter which one, so long as he reached the log first.

Fargo was almost there when the footsteps behind him flurried faster, then suddenly stopped altogether. Exactly why became apparent when a heavy form smashed into his hips and brawny arms encircled his waist. He was brought down less than two feet from the rifles and pistols.

It was the Ute with the long knife. Fargo dodged a swipe that nearly split his face, parried a thrust at his stomach, and whipped an elbow into the warrior's throat. The man's grip slackened. Sputtering, the Ute drew back, allowing Fargo to hook a knee into the warrior's chest and batter him aside.

The weapons were so close, Fargo could almost reach out and touch them. Using his knees as fulcrums, he levered himself forward. His outflung hand closed on his Colt. As he twisted, an arrow missed his head by a finger's width.

The Ute with the long knife rose, swept the blade overhead, and leaped.

Fargo fired as the man swooped down. The slug cored the warrior's brain and snapped him to one side. Without missing a beat, Fargo swiveled to shoot again, this time at Tall Bear and the Ute with the bow. Neither were where they had been. Bounding like mule deer, they were in full flight toward the trees.

Fargo adopted a two-handed grip and tracked Tall Bear. As his finger tightened, the warrior swerved. The bullet missed. A couple of long strides were all Tall Bear needed to gain cover. Fargo sat up to take deliberate aim, but the clash had taken more out of him than he had realized. His limbs went weak. It was all he could do to hold the Colt, let alone point it.

Tall Bear and his companion melted into the firs.

Laughter filled the clearing. Ike McDermott walked over, slapping his leg in glee. "That was some scrape, sonny! I haven't been so entertained since the time I saw the Utes and the Navajos tussle over the hot springs!"

Fargo wasn't amused. "Thanks for lending me a hand," he declared bitterly. Morning Flower came up alongside the prospector and Fargo glared at her, as well. "You, too, lady."

The woman bowed her head, unable to look him in the eyes.

"Now, hold your horses there, sonny," McDermott scolded. "She didn't help you because I wouldn't let her. She wanted to, but I grabbed onto her leg so she couldn't go anywhere."

The weakness was gone from Fargo's arms and legs. Slowly sitting up, he began reloading the Colt on the off chance the two Utes might come back. "I suppose you thought that you were doing me a favor by not lifting a finger," he told McDermott.

The prospector was unruffled. "Not you, sonny, us. Morning Flower is already in enough hot water with her people. If she had killed one of those braves just to save a white man, her tribe would never forgive her. She'd be worse off than she already is."

Fargo hated to admit it, but the half-pint had a point. "What about you? Afraid the Utes wouldn't let you prospect in their territory any more if you put windows in the skull of one of their warriors?"

McDermott nodded briskly. "That's it exactly! I'm glad to see that you appreciate the fact. I can't do anything to jeopardize their trust. Hope you'll forgive me."

Fargo was inclined to do anything but. Yet it was flattering to know that Morning Flower had wanted to aid him. She was staring at her feet, crestfallen. "Sorry I growled at you," he apologized. "And I hope Tall Bear won't be able to stir up more trouble for you because of me."

The prospector replied, not her. "I'm afraid that's exactly what the weasel will do. He'll call a meeting of the council and demand that they send a war party to rub you out. And while he's at it, he'll try to convince them that something should be done about her." McDermott stooped to collect his revolvers. "He'll go on and on about how it's an insult to the whole tribe for her to be living off by herself and taking in every white stray she comes across. Knowing Tall Bear, he'll make a pitch for her to be his woman and make it seem as if it's in the tribe's best interests. He's crafty, that one is."

Morning Flower's silence confirmed McDermott's prediction. Fargo felt like a fool for having lit into her the way he had, and even worse because he had brought the wrath of her people down on her head. Somehow, he had to make it up to her. He owed her his life.

To the prospector, Fargo said, "I don't want any harm coming to her on my account. You know the Utes better than I do. Care to give me any advice?"

McDermott stared in the direction Tall Bear had taken.

"First thing is to get the hell out of here. We have to pack up everything, the lodge and all."

"And go where?" Fargo wanted to know. Eluding the Utes would be next to impossible. That region was their home. They knew it better than any white man ever could.

Ike McDermott nodded toward Treasure Mountain. "Short of hightailing it for the plains, there's only one place where we might be safe."

"You know of somewhere we can lay low?"

"I do, sonny. But . . ." McDermott gnawed on his lower lip, then shrugged. "I reckon it can't be helped. Cross that bridge when I get there."

"What?"

"Nothing," McDermott said, averting his gaze. "Let's get cracking, shall we? And keep your eyes skinned. I wouldn't put it past Tall Bear to leave his other friend behind to keep watch on us."

They were hampered by the rapidly dwindling light. Soon it was too dark to pack by so the prospector built a fire near the horses while Fargo saddled the Ovaro and threw an Ute saddle on the mare. Shortly afterward, McDermott skipped off into the brush to the north. He returned with his mount and a donkey in tow, whistling softly to himself, not the least bit flustered by the turn of events.

Fargo had just tied down his bedroll. He turned, and thought he was seeing things. Stupefied, he moved to meet McDermott halfway. "Where in the world?" he exclaimed.

The prospector's mount was the smallest horse Fargo had ever seen. It was so small, that Fargo half thought it must be a foal. But on looking closer, he saw that it was indeed a mature animal, a superbly built pony a third smaller than any pony he knew of. It was as black as pitch with a brilliant blaze on its brow.

"Isn't he a beauty?" McDermott said. "I call him Nightwind. He's as surefooted as a mountain goat and as fast as your pinto over a short stretch." He stroked the pony and kissed its muzzle. "I wouldn't part with him for all the ore in Treasure Mountain."

"Where did you find him?"

Nightwind nuzzled the prospector, enjoying the attention. "Texas, believe it or not. I've always heard that everyone and everything grows twice as big there. But in San Antonio I saw a man leading Nightwind down the street, and it was love at first sight. I had to have him no matter what the cost." McDermott laughed. "I badgered that fella for days, pestered him day and night, and plumb wore him down to a frazzle. It cost me practically all the money I had at the time, but Nightwind was worth it."

Morning Flower came out of the tepee lugging several parfleches crammed with her effects. Fargo hurried to help her. She was so deep in thought that she jumped when he laid a hand on her arm.

"I didn't mean to spook you."

She gave him a parfleche without comment. As they crossed to her mare, she cleared her throat. "You do not need to do this. Go while you have the chance."

"What kind of man would run out on a woman at a time like this?" Fargo said.

"You are not in my debt. What I did for you, I would have done for anyone."

Fargo smirked. "And what I'm doing for you, I'd do for any beautiful woman who risked her pretty hide to save mine."

Morning Flower actually blushed. "I am not so beautiful."

"Looked in a mirror lately?" Fargo shot back. "I'll bet your Joe would agree that you are downright gorgeous." He saw it had been a mistake to mention her late husband when she gazed off into the forest to hide her haunted expression.

Working together, the three of them took another half an hour to get everything ready to go. Fargo had been curious how Morning Flower transported her belongings, and he learned the answer when she walked behind the lodge and reappeared dragging a small travois.

Many mountain and prairie tribes relied on them. Two long poles were lashed together at one end to form an A-shaped drag. Close to the other end a wide lattice-type platform was attached, sturdy enough to bear many hundreds of pounds.

The Ute woman did not have anywhere near that much. She strapped down all her possessions, then covered them with one of the elk hides used on her lodge. As she stepped to the high-bowed buckskin saddle, Fargo offered a hand to give her a boost.

She hesitated.

"I won't drop you. I promise."

Morning Flower let herself be hoisted up. Her dress swirled, revealing a hint of silken inner thigh. She adjusted the hem and lifted the reins.

Fargo mounted. It was dangerous to be riding in the mountains at night but it was essential they get a big lead on Tall Bear. Since the others knew the lay of the land, he was content to bring up the rear. They forded at a gravel bar and pushed into the undergrowth. Fargo looked over a shoulder as the brush closed around them and spotted a shadowy shape moving across the clearing.

McDermott had hit the nail on the head.

One of the Utes was stalking them.

6

For the moment, Skye Fargo said nothing to his two companions. It suited his purpose to have the Ute believe no one had detected him, so he rode on, pretending not to have noticed their shadow.

Navigating rugged mountainous terrain at night was always a risky proposition. Obstacles were often not spotted until the last moment. There were ruts and sinkholes and animal burrows to watch out for, as well as the many great predators which roamed in search of prey after the sun went down. Rattlesnakes, too, did most of their hunting after dark, and a rider never knew when the harsh rattle of one of the slithering reptiles might send his mount into a mindless panic.

Fargo kept his eyes peeled as the prospector led them along a winding game trail between two hills and up over a low ridge. Every so often he would check on the Ute on the sly. Twice he glimpsed the warrior, far back. The man rode a dun, its light coat a sharp contrast to the inky background.

As McDermott started down the ridge, Fargo spurred the Ovaro, passing the travois and slowing between Morning Flower and the prospector so both could hear him when he announced, "One of Tall Bear's friends is playing follow the leader. When the time is right, I'll deal with him. In the meantime, don't let on that you know he's back there."

"Will do," McDermott said, tugging on the lead rope to his donkey.

It felt strange to Fargo, talking down to a grown man on a pony that came no higher than the stallion's belly. He went to rein around to return to the rear of the line.

"There's a spot I know of," McDermott mentioned.

"About a mile yonder we'll pass through a small valley choked with aspens. That would be as good a place as any."

"I'll be ready," Fargo said. Again he began to turn but Morning Flower stopped him by saying his name.

"Be very careful," she advised. "The warrior who follows us has slain many enemies. He likes to kill up close, with a knife. In our tongue, his name means Lightning Hands." She glanced toward the top of the ridge. "He is not afraid of anything, man or beast. Many winters ago, well before I met my Joe, he courted me, but I found him too arrogant. Almost as bad as Tall Bear himself."

Fargo digested the news while falling back. It put the warrior's actions in a whole new light. Fargo had figured the man was just plain careless about being seen, but Lightning Hands apparently didn't give a damn whether they knew he was there or not. It was almost as if the warrior had thrown down a gauntlet, in effect saying, "I am following you, and I dare you to do anything about it."

Well, Fargo was going to take up that gauntlet. He didn't glance around again until they had covered another half a mile. Sure enough, Lightning Hands was right on their trail, out in the open, making no attempt to hide.

A knobby spine that inclined downward hundreds of feet in a span of minutes brought them to the valley McDermott had told Fargo about. Aspens had long since overgrown most of the valley floor, crowding up close to a ribbon of a stream. McDermott guided them along the west bank, where enough grass remained to make the going easy.

The stream angled to the northwest. No sooner was Fargo around the bend than he reined up. Morning Flower glanced back at him and he smiled to reassure her. Her answering smile did not share his confidence.

Not having any time to spare, Fargo entered the aspens. A dozen yards in, he reined up, slid down, and looped the reins around a slender bole. Pulling the Henry from the boot, he hurried to the edge of the trees and sank to his right knee at a spot affording a clear view of the bend.

McDermott and Morning Flower were almost out of sight. The warrior would be there at any moment. Fargo pressed the rifle stock against his shoulder and sighted on the point where Lightning Hands should appear.

Tense seconds elapsed. Fargo emptied his head of all distracting thoughts. He had to stay ready and focused. There would only be one opportunity. If he missed with his first shot, the Ute was not going to sit there and let him shoot again.

The seconds became a full minute. Then two. Fargo sensed that something was wrong. The Ute should have been there by then. He lifted his eyes from the barrel to the grass strip bordering the stream. A third minute went by, and still the warrior did not show.

The only explanation Fargo could think of was that the man had decided to skirt the valley and pick them up on the other side. That's what a cautious man would do, at any rate. But Lightning Hands didn't care one bit about being seen.

Maybe, Fargo mused, the Ute knew another way through the aspens. A shorter way than following the stream. Fargo tilted his head to listen for the drum of hooves but the only sound was the constant rustling of aspen leaves.

The wind had grown stronger, as it invariably did in the mountains at night, and would not let up until near dawn.

Fargo waited another two minutes. At last, convinced that the Ute wasn't coming, he rose, let down the hammer on the Henry, and hurried toward the Ovaro. If the warrior had somehow slipped past him, he had to overtake the prospector and the woman quickly. There was no telling what a bloodthirsty character like Lightning Hands would do.

The stallion was staring off into the trees. Fargo looked but saw nothing. He faced the pinto, the Henry cradled in the crook of his left elbow. Suddenly a shadow seemed to detach itself from the other shadows and hurtle at him. A glint of metal in the starlight confirmed that it wasn't a trick of his imagination.

The Ute had guessed what he would do and slipped into the aspens to catch him unawares.

Fargo spun, but he was a hair too late. The knife descended. It would have sliced into his chest if not for the

Henry, for as he pivoted, the barrel struck the Ute's wrist a glancing blow, hard enough to deflect the swing. Fargo backpedaled and gripped the Henry with both hands to bring it to bear.

The Ute was not about to let him. Silently, grimly, the warrior pressed in close and thrust, down low. Fargo parried the blade with the Henry, then was forced to do so again and again as the Ute stabbed and thrust without letup, never giving him a moment's respite.

The next second Fargo bumped into an aspen. He skipped to the left as the knife nearly sheared off an ear. The blade hit the tree instead, biting deep. Lightning Hands had to tug it free to renew his attack.

It was the opening Fargo needed. He began to raise the Henry. Anxious to end the fight, he didn't think to look behind him. His left heel snagged on something. Before he could help himself, Fargo fell, landing on his back. He swiveled and pointed the rifle at the spot where the warrior had just been, only Lightning Hands was no longer there.

The Ute had vanished.

Fargo pushed to his knees, hunched low in case the warrior threw the knife at him. Nothing moved among the tightly spaced slender trunks. He glanced at the Ovaro, thinking the stallion might give him a clue as to which direction the warrior had gone, but the pinto was staring at him, not after the Ute.

Off to the south, another horse nickered lightly.

That would be Lightning Hands's animal, Fargo knew. He looked to see if he could spot it, and as he turned his head, the air hummed to the passage of a streaking arrow. It glanced off a tree behind him. Flattening, Fargo crawled to the right, putting more trees between him and the Ute. Another shaft zipped wide of the mark.

For a while after that all was quiet. Fargo scoured the aspens but it was as if he battled a ghost. Lightning Hands was invisible.

Fargo planned to let the Ute make the next move. Patience was called for, and he lay there for the longest while, his finger on the trigger. He didn't hear the warrior's animal again.

Fargo would have been content to stay there for as long as it took to draw the Ute into the open. Then the Ovaro took a step toward him, alerting him to two dangers. One was that the stallion would inadvertently give him away, the other that the Ute might take it into his crafty head to put a few arrows into the pinto to leave Fargo stranded afoot.

Slowly rising, but staying low to the ground, Fargo circled to the right to come up on the stallion from the side. To his annoyance, the Ovaro turned as he turned.

If Lightning Hands were watching, the Ute would know exactly where Fargo was.

The big man halted. He scanned the aspens, dug his toes into the ground, then shot toward the stallion as if catapulted from a cannon. Hardly was he in motion when a humming shaft nearly brushed his right ear. He weaved, and weaved again. Another arrow nicked his hat. It came from a thick patch of aspens off to the left so he worked the Henry twice, firing into the heart of the cluster, not really expecting to put a slug into his enemy but hoping to keep the warrior pinned down long enough to mount.

In another bound Fargo was at the stallion. Shoving the rifle into the saddle scabbard, he grabbed the horn and vaulted up. As he straightened, the Colt blossomed in his right hand. He squeezed off a pair of shots at the same spot while wheeling the stallion.

Yet another shaft sought his life, but this one came from a different direction. Lightning Hands had changed position.

Fargo squeezed off one more shot. A jab of his spurs goaded the Ovaro into flight but the trees were packed so close together that the best the pinto could manage was a brisk walk.

Something moved, to the right. Fargo banged away at the very instant that a bow string twanged. The arrow nearly nicked his gun hand. He fired again, driving the shape to ground.

A clearing appeared. Ground-hitched in the center was the dun. Fargo grinned as he veered toward it, snatched its reins on the fly, and plunged into the aspens on the other side.

A howl of outrage split the air.

For a man who was supposed to be partial to knives, Lightning Hands relied on his bow a lot. From out of nowhere flashed an arrow that thudded into the Ovaro's side. The stallion whinnied in pain, and Fargo's first thought was that a vital organ had been hit.

Trees closed around them. Fargo kept on riding, since to stop invited an arrow between the shoulder blades. He checked, but the Ute was too clever to charge across the clearing after him.

Once enough ground had been covered that Fargo judged it safe, he drew rein and hopped down. The shaft had caught the pinto down low at an angle, the tip passing through the stirrup leather and the fender. Fargo lifted the fender, afraid to find blood, but the arrowhead had not gone clean through the skirt. It was wedged tight in the leather, so tight that he had to twist and turn before it worked itself out.

Relieved, Fargo broke the arrow in half and threw it down. He ran a hand over the stallion's side to verify there was no wound.

Back among the aspens Fargo had just passed through, a twig snapped.

Fargo wasted no time climbing on and heading out. The dun balked every so often, but a strong yank on its reins always persuaded it to continue. Fargo reached the base of a steep slope and climbed. Here the aspens thinned, enabling him to cover his own back.

Presently the Ovaro stepped onto a narrow shelf. Deer tracks crossed it, leading to a game trail that paralleled the valley. It wasn't long before Fargo came to the valley mouth. He thought that the prospector and the woman would be long gone, but there they were, waiting where the valley blended into a jagged row of mountains.

"I know, I know," McDermott said as Fargo drew near. "We should have been long gone by now, but this sweet gal wouldn't go a step farther without you." His grin was fit for a shark. "Darned if I know why."

Morning Flower stared at the dun. "Lightning Hands?" she asked.

"Still alive, sorry to say," Fargo responded. "But unless he can sprout wings and fly, he won't be showing up any time soon."

McDermott laughed. "Knowing that wildcat as I do, he'll take the loss of his horse mighty personal. Don't be surprised if he hunts you to the ends of the earth to erase the insult." Clucking to Nightwind, he got them on their way.

Fargo rode beside Morning Flower. "I appreciate your concern, but you don't need to fret on my account. I can look out for myself."

It was hard to read her expression in the dark. She seemed to become melancholy. "My Joe said the same thing. Many times. And look at what happened."

"Ask any poker player. A person never knows when the cards will turn against them. The best we can do is play the hand we're dealt and hope for the best."

Morning Flower looked at him. "What is this thing you talk about, poker?"

"A card game," Fargo explained. She shook her head to show that she still didn't understand. "I take it that your Joe wasn't a gambling man?"

"What is gambling?"

Fargo chuckled. "Games of chance, we call them. I have a pack in my saddlebags. Remind me to teach you if we ever have the time."

"I would like that very much."

They pushed on, bearing to the northeast, Fargo again bringing up the rear. From time to time he surveyed the countryside behind them, and not once did he note any sign of pursuit.

Several hours of hard riding brought them to a creek. McDermott entered the water and turned Nightwind upstream in the very middle. "This is Treasure Creek," he declared, "where I first struck color. We'll follow it for a spell. Stay away from either shore and any gravel bars we encounter to avoid leaving tracks."

Fargo knew what to do. It was a trick as old as the hills they had passed through earlier. By sticking to the center of the stream, they insured that within a few short hours the swift current would obliterate every trace of their passage.

It would be impossible for the Utes to track them from that point on.

The only hitch was that they had to leave the water sometime, and wherever they did, they would leave prints. Brushing out the tracks with a handful of weeds or a tree limb wouldn't fool the Utes since doing so left marks every bit as obvious as the tracks themselves.

The breeze grew cooler. They had been climbing steadily for hours and now they climbed even more steeply, up the lower slopes of vast Treasure Mountain. Ike McDermott rode with confidence. Plainly, he had been this way many times before. He knew where every gravel bar was, knew where low limbs posed obstacles. Thanks to him they were able to travel swiftly.

The air grew colder still. Treasure Mountain reared well over eleven thousand feet above sea level. While by no means the highest in the Rockies, it was an imposing peak, majestic in sweep, stark at the summit, which was crowned with snow.

The higher they climbed, the faster the current flowed. Thankfully the water was shallow more often than not or their horses would have been scrambling for purchase on the slippery rocks lining the creek bed.

As it was, when a short series of naturally formed stone steps barred their way, Morning Flower's dun nearly lost its footing. Burdened by the travois, it could not move as nimbly as the other animals. As it scrambled up over the lip of one of the wide steps, its rear legs flailed madly. It tottered, on the verge of spilling its rider and crashing onto its side.

Fargo spurred to her assistance. Moving up beside the mare, he tucked his left leg up under him and angled the Ovaro against her mount so that the two animals pressed against one another, the stallion bracing the smaller horse to prevent it from falling.

That was all Morning Flower needed. In seconds she had the mare on a solid footing. Smiling, she said, "Thank you for your help. We are even now, as whites like to say."

"Like hell we are," Fargo disagreed. "Saving you from a bad spill doesn't begin to repay you for saving my life."

A high-pitched whistle interrupted them. McDermott had

drawn rein about thirty yards further and was waiting for them to catch up. When they did, the prospector slanted to the left, to a flat stone spine jutting halfway into the water. "Once you're out, stay on rocky ground," he directed.

It wasn't hard to do. The spine was just a small spur on a massive slab of solid stone that extended over a wide area for as far as the eye could see. Fargo had to hand it to the prospector. They wouldn't leave a single track. If the Utes came that far, the warriors would have no idea where they had left the stream. It was a trick worthy of Fargo himself.

But the best was yet to come.

McDermott led them up a short slope to a stone shelf broad enough for all of their horses to stand end to end. He made straight for a low cliff, for the heavy brush and trees growing at its base.

Fargo figured the prospector would halt at any moment. To his amazement, McDermott rode into the brush, past a wide pine, and was gone. It was as if the man had ridden *into* the cliff.

Morning Flower acted every bit as flabbergasted as Fargo. Gaping, she halted.

"McDermott?" Fargo called out. No answer was forthcoming, so he moved past her into the growth. Weeds as high as his knees brushed against him as he went around the same pine the prospector had passed. A puff of cool wind blew on his face, and before his wondering gaze a huge dark cavity materialized. It was the mouth of a cave! Around a kink in a short tunnel, light flared.

A dozen feet more and Fargo found himself in a spacious chamber illuminated by a torch McDermott had just lit. The prospector moved to another and applied a burning brand. The walls and ceiling were promptly bathed in their combined glow.

"What do you think, sonny?" McDermott asked.

For one of the few times ever in his life, Skye Fargo was speechless. The cave was much larger than he had thought, extending well beyond the dancing torchlight. Overhead, a magnificent arched ceiling crowned the high walls. But what astounded Fargo the most wasn't the cavern's immense size. More dazzling were the bands of glittering ore that lined the walls and the ceiling, bands of pure silver, more silver than he or any other man except McDermott had ever seen in one place at one time, enough silver to make the man who found it the richest person alive.

A ragged hole along the right-hand wall revealed where McDermott had been mining. Nuggets the size of hen's eggs littered the floor around the cavity.

McDermott took one of the torches from its bracket and held it aloft for Fargo to see better. "Isn't it a sight, though?" he said, and chortled. "The first time I set eyes on this, I had to smack myself twice to make sure I wasn't imagining things."

"Now I know why Wolf Rollins is after you," Fargo said. "He must suspect the truth."

"That jackass?" McDermott snorted. "He thinks I've struck a small vein somewhere. No one other than you, absolutely no one, knows the truth."

From the mouth of the tunnel, Morning Flower corrected the prospector. "I know," she said. Nudging the mare into the main chamber, she scanned the walls and frowned. "What is so special about the shiny metal that white men will kill for it? It is too soft to make a good knife blade, too heavy to carry a lot of it at a time." She dismounted. "My people have never thought that silver is much good for anything."

"Begging your pardon, missy," McDermott said, "but your people are still running around with bows and arrows when truly civilized men carry guns. The Utes have a long way to go before they catch up to the rest of the world." Sliding the torch back into the bracket, he stepped to his pony. "This shiny metal, as you call it, means I am wealthy beyond belief. It's power, too, because a wealthy man can do as he damn well pleases and not have to worry about the consequences."

"You crave power over your fellow white men?" Morning Flower asked.

McDermott leaned on Nightwind. "Not power so much as an equal footing." He motioned at the nearest shimmering band. "I'll be able to do whatever I want, when I want. My size will no longer matter. I can deal with others on my own terms, rather than having to do as they want just because they are bigger than me."

Fargo slid from the saddle, pondering. Anyone else would have been deliriously happy at merely finding that much ore, but the prospector saw it as a means to an end, as a way to lord it over those who had always looked down their noses at him on account of his height. "For your sake, McDermott, I hope word of your strike never leaks out."

"Oh, I'm sure it won't," the man said. He stepped back from the pony, holding his Sharps. Pivoting to cover them, he said, "And the reason I'm so sure is because neither of you are ever going to tell another soul."

7

Morning Flower started toward the midget. "What is the meaning of this? My Joe and you were good friends. And you have always been welcome at my lodge."

Ike McDermott had the Sharps fixed on Fargo. Shifting, he wagged it at her to stop her in her tracks. "Now is hardly the time for explanations, my dear. Suffice it to say that I regret what must be done, but I have no choice." He covered Fargo again.

Lying next to a nearby wall were many of the tools of McDermott's trade, among them two shovels and a pick. A coiled rope had been placed beside them. The prospector nodded at it and said to the Ute, "I want you to tie up the big man here, good and tight."

"And if I refuse?" Morning Flower asked. "Will you shoot me down like you would a rabid dog?"

McDermott angrily stamped a foot. "Why are you giving me such a hard time? I'm only doing what I have to. You should be grateful I don't kill him." He sighted on Fargo's leg. "But so help me, if you don't do as I say right this minute, I'll blow one of his kneecaps clean off."

Fargo had been as taken aback by the turn of events as the Ute. Never once in the ten hours or so they had been together had McDermott done anything to indicate he might turn on them. Fargo had assumed the prospector was Morning Flower's close friend, and had taken it for granted that he helped them mainly on her account. Yet here the man was, pointing a gun at her and bossing her around.

Morning Flower reluctantly fetched the rope. At McDermott's insistence, she steered Fargo to a spot where folded blankets were stacked. McDermott made her relieve Fargo of the Colt and the toothpick. Then she bound Fargo's wrists, the prospector watching her every move. About done, she leaned close to Fargo's ear to say softly, "I am very sorry. I do not want to do this, but I believe he really will shoot you if I do not."

"I guess you don't know him as well as you thought that you did," Fargo responded.

"He has always been so kind," Morning Flower said, and opened her mouth to say more when McDermott barked at them.

"Enough jawing! Move back, girl, so I can see if you did a proper job!" He warily approached, examined the knots carefully, and visibly relaxed. Lowering the Sharps, he took a seat on a small rectangular boulder a few feet away. Close to it were the charred embers of a fire. "Well, now that that's out of the way, what do you two say to a cup of coffee? I'll even do the honors."

"How generous of you," Fargo said flatly.

McDermott propped the Sharps on the boulder and rose to retrieve a coffee pot. "Now, now, sonny," he said. "Keep a civil tongue. I haven't hurt you any, have I? You're still alive, aren't you?"

"For how long?" Fargo bluntly asked.

The prospector, reaching for a water skin, paused. "Is that what you think? That I'd murder you in cold blood? Lord Almighty! What kind of man do you take me for?"

"The kind who just threatened to put a hole in my knee," Fargo answered, and bobbed his head at the woman. "The kind who would turn on a good friend for no reason whatsoever."

McDermott chuckled. "What's a little hole in the leg compared to one in the head, eh? I swear! Some folks never know when they're well off. All they can do is gripe!"

Fargo could tell the man was serious, yet that only mystified him more. It made him wonder if maybe finding so much silver had taken a toll on McDermott's mental state. The man wouldn't be the first. Lust for wealth had turned many a good man bad. Greed often made men do things they wouldn't ordinarily do.

Morning Flower sat primly on another small boulder. "I would like to know why you have done this, Ike."

"It's all around you, my dear," McDermott said, pointing at a band of ore.

"You are afraid Fargo will kill you to get his hands on your shiny metal?"

McDermott arched an eye at Skye. "He doesn't seem the kind, does he? But then, I don't know him all that well. I can't take the chance of him slipping that pigsticker of his into my back."

Morning Flower appeared as confused as Fargo. "If you felt this way all along, why did you bring him here?"

"Why else? For your sake, dearie. You and that husband of yours always treated me decently. You never looked down your noses at me like most people your size do." McDermott gathered an armload of dead wood from a large pile of busted branches he had previously collected. "I couldn't let Tall Bear run roughshod over you. You needed somewhere safe to hide, and this is the safest place I know of." He surveyed the cavern fondly. "No one knows about it except the three of us. Tall Bear will never find you."

Fargo had been testing the rope binding his wrists. Morning Flower had looped it tight, but not so tight that he couldn't wriggle free in time. In addition, the last of the knots she had tied was slightly loose, enough so that he could pry at it with a fingernail. "What if I gave you my word that I would never tell anyone about your strike?" he asked the prospector. "Would you let me go?"

"Your word?" McDermott snickered. "You must think I'm plumb crazy. No, sonny. I can't let you leave. And I won't kill you, either, unless you give me cause."

"Then what's your plan?" Fargo asked. "Do you aim to keep me here until you've mined every last ounce of silver?" It was a sarcastic question, the last thing in the world Fargo would expect a sane man to consider doing. Yet the prospector grinned and nodded.

"You're a smart one, I'll say that for you."

Fargo looked at all the glittering veins in the walls and the vaulted ceiling. "It would take ten lifetimes to mine all this ore."

McDermott was arranging the firewood on top of the embers of his last fire. "You'd better hope it doesn't take that long or you'll never see the outside world again."

Morning Flower had been quiet for a while, lost in thought. Now she spoke up. "What you are doing is wrong, Ike. I can not be a party to it."

"I'm afraid you don't have any choice," McDermott said. "I can't let you leave, either."

"What will you do if I try? Shoot me in the knee as you would Fargo?"

The prospector pursed his lips. "No, I could never harm a hair on your head. But I know how fond you are of that mare of yours. And I don't have any qualms about putting a few holes in it."

For a while after that, no one uttered a word. McDermott, whistling to himself, got the fire going and placed the coffee pot on to boil. Next he picked up his rifle and walked over to the cavity in the wall, saying, "Behave yourselves, now! Don't make me do anything I'll regret."

The whole time Fargo had been working on his bonds. He had wriggled his wrists back and forth without being obvious about it and gained a little slack. He had also succeeded in partially untying the first knot. When McDermott rose, he had to stop. The cavity was directly behind him.

Morning Flower stared at the strange little man, and frowned. "Many winters have I known him. He was friends with my Joe before Joe even met me. I could not count the times we made him welcome, the times we shared our meat with him. Yet I can see now that I never truly knew this man." She paused. "He is not the person I thought he was."

Loud blows rang out. McDermott had taken a pick to a vein. He paid them no mind when they looked around.

"Did your husband have any interest in prospecting?" Fargo asked.

"None," Morning Flower said. "He liked being a trapper. I heard him tell Ike that he was wasting his time roaming the mountains in search of the silver metal. A fool's proposition, he called it."

"Maybe that's why Ike liked him," Fargo guessed. "Your

husband was the one man Ike didn't have to worry would try to steal his claim."

Morning Flower grew somber. "I never thought of it that way. How sad, if true. The silver metal must mean more than life itself to him."

Fargo shifted. The prospector was fondling a large chunk of ore as if it were a woman's breast. "I'd say that's about the size of things," he said.

McDermott laughed lightly and held the silver out for them to admire. "Talk about me all you want, but it won't change my way of thinking one bit. Hell, sonny, if the boot was on the other foot, I bet you'd do just as I'm doing. You wouldn't trust a living soul."

"Being rich isn't all there is to life," Fargo commented.

Ike McDermott blinked, then roared with mirth. He laughed so hard that he rocked back on his boot heels. Tears poured down over his ruddy cheeks into his beard. Cackling and slapping his thigh, he went on and on until he was drained dry. Gasping, he clutched his side, then swiped a hand at the corners of his eyes. "Where did you ever get a tomfool notion like that? *You're* the one who is touched in the head, if you ask me." Rising, he shook the ore at them. "Money and power! Nothing else matters in this old world of ours!"

Fargo was not going to waste breath arguing the point. McDermott was downright fanatical in his lust for the precious ore, and no amount of talking would ever change his outlook.

Soon steam hissed from the coffee pot. Morning Flower filled three tin cups. Kneeling in front of Fargo, she lifted one to his lips so he could take a sip.

McDermott joined them, grinning. "If I didn't know better, my dear, I'd swear that you've taken a shine to this tall drink of water."

Morning Flower glared and started to rise.

"Hold on, gal," McDermott exclaimed lightheartedly. "I'm not saying it's wrong or anything. Fact is, you've been alone too damn long. It's about time you showed an interest in another man." Helping himself to one of the cups, he hunkered down and took a loud sip. "Ahhh. Six or seven of these and I should make it through the day with no problem."

Fargo renewed his assault on the rope. His fingers flew, and in moments he succeeded in unraveling the first knot. As he applied himself to the second, he happened to glance toward the tunnel. The weary horses were right where they had been left standing, but something about them was wrong. He studied each animal, trying to make sense of his gut feeling. Then it hit him. "It's gone," he declared.

McDermott, about to take another swallow, hesitated. "What's that, sonny?"

"A horse has strayed off," Fargo said.

Twisting, the prospector indicated each animal in turn. "There's Nightwind, my donkey Gertrude, your big pinto, and Morning Flower's mare. All are accounted for. So what are you trying to pull?"

"I never claimed it was one of ours," Fargo clarified. "It's the dun that is missing."

"Damn!" McDermott thundered, leaping to his feet. "Lightning Hands's horse! If it wanders on back down the mountain, it'll leave a clear trail for the Utes to follow! They'll be here before we know it." Throwing down his cup, he was all set to rush off when he caught himself and swung to face them. "What am I doing? I can't leave the two of you alone. Morning Flower will untie you the minute I'm gone."

Fargo saw his chance slipping away. "You can't let the dun get very far, either. Every second you stay here makes it that much more likely that the Utes will find your cavern."

Torn by indecision, McDermott gnawed on his lower lip while glancing from them to the tunnel and back again. "This is a hell of a note!" he growled. "I reckon there's only one thing to be done."

Morning Flower was unprepared for what happened next. She cried out as McDermott pounced on her and wrenched her arms behind her back. Although she resisted, he tied her wrists without any problem. Her ankles were next. She kicked at him but he simply sat on her legs, pinning them long enough to get the job done.

Holding the last length of rope, McDermott came toward Fargo. "Now your ankles, sonny. And don't give me a hard time or I'll knock you out and do it anyway."

Fargo suppressed a smile. "Don't worry. I know when I'm licked." He sat quietly as the prospector wrapped the rope around his legs three times and made two large knots.

"There! That should hold you!" McDermott said. Hustling to the horses, he mounted Nightwind. "Behave yourselves," he said as he departed, the Sharps across his thighs.

The instant they were alone, Fargo slid off the boulder and hunched like an oversized snail to the fire. Rather than spend precious moments wrestling with the knots, he turned so his back was to the flames. Gingerly, he held his wrists as close as he dared. The heat was intense. He glanced over his shoulder, selected a low flame at the edge, and positioned the rope above it. The hemp blackened and crinkled. Pain coursed up both arms but he didn't give up. A few charred strands parted. Then a few more.

Morning Flower, doing her part without being told, glued her gaze to the tunnel.

Fargo rotated his wrists to reduce some of the searing discomfort. They were red from the heat and slick with sweat. He could move both hands, but not yet enough to slip loose. Girding himself, he lowered the rope into the flames. A loud crackling and hissing confirmed the hemp had caught fire, just as the sharp pangs that ran up his arms confirmed he was close to frying his flesh to a crisp.

When Fargo could endure the pain no longer, he jerked his arms out. The movement caused the rope to slide off. He was free at last! Bending to untie his ankles, he discovered that his left wrist was badly blistered. His right was not quite as bad, but oddly enough, it hurt more.

Morning Flower took one look and said, "I have herbs that will relieve the pain and help you heal. They are in one of my parfleches. All I need do is heat some water first."

"Later," Fargo said, tugging at a stubborn knot. "After we're in the clear."

"But you must be—" Morning Flower began.

Fargo cut her off with a gesture. "There's no telling how long McDermott will be gone. Maybe the dun didn't stray all that far." The knot came apart. He tugged at the next. "We need to be long gone when he gets back."

"He will come after us."

"His mistake," Fargo said. "I won't let him hog-tie me a second time."

In under three minutes they were on their feet. Fargo immediately reclaimed his hardware and the Arkansas toothpick. He handed Morning Flower's rifle and ammo pouch up to her after she climbed on the mare. "I'll check outside while you turn the travois around," he proposed.

Leading the stallion, Fargo hastened to the cave entrance. Through the brush he could see the rock shelf but not much else. Leaving the stallion in deep shadow, he crept into the open. Overhead, a multitude of stars sparkled. A sliver of moon hung low to the west. To the east, the first pink tinge of dawn heralded the beginning of a new day.

From the rim Fargo scoured the murky landscape below. Since they had climbed over halfway up the mountain, he enjoyed a panoramic vista. Dense tracts of forest were broken by meadows and fields. No movement was evident, but that meant nothing. McDermott might be anywhere.

Returning to the cavern, Fargo forked leather as Morning Flower appeared. Without comment she trailed him to the north rim, stopping when he did.

"I think we should leave my travois here. It will slow us down too much."

"Next to everything you own is on it," Fargo said. "We'll haul it along for as long as we can." A nudge of his heels sent the Ovaro over the edge. As they had done before, he made for the creek and rode out into the middle. It was fitting that he use the prospector's own ruse against him.

Instead of turning south, back the way they had come, Fargo reined to the north. He had a plan, such as it was. McDermott, no doubt, was lower down on Treasure Mountain. To avoid him, Fargo intended to go up and over the top, then descend the far side. The prospector would never expect them to try such a stunt, not hauling a travois.

And since the Utes would probably approach from the south, heading north made twice as much sense.

Gradually, the sky brightened. The woodland came alive

with the chirping of birds and the chattering of squirrels and chipmunks.

Fargo twisted frequently to scan the lower slopes. No one appeared. By the middle of the morning they were above the tree line. Here the creek was deep and swift. In spots it was a torrent, frothing with rapids. When the roughest stretch yet unfolded before them, he decided enough was enough.

Slanting onto the left bank, Fargo halted. Before them an alpine meadow flanked a jagged low ridge. A lone hawk soared above it, in search of prey.

The mare slipped when she reached the bank. Morning Flower had to lash the reins and smack her legs against the animal in order to urge it onward. Just as the mare came to the top, the travois caught on a submerged rock. Drawing up short, the mare whinnied, then strained. The travois would not budge.

"Let me take a look," Fargo said, sliding down. He waded in, the cold water rapidly rising. When it bubbled around the tops of his boots, he stopped. From where he stood, it was apparent the travois would not work itself loose. He had to go further.

Morning Flower was worried. "You might slip and fall in if you keep going. I will cut the travois free."

"No," Fargo said. "We've brought it this far. We're not quitting now." On the lookout for rocks that could trip him, he ventured closer. Freezing water soaked his socks and his feet. In moments it felt as if he had stuck both feet into a bucket of ice.

Fargo grabbed hold of the long pole on his side and alternated between pressing down and pulling up. The travois rocked but not enough to free it. He edged past the latticework and tried again with the same result.

Incredibly strong current tugged at Fargo's legs. Placing each foot down as if he were treading on eggshells, he moved to the rear of the drag and rocked furiously, using his whole body for leverage. The travois moved a few inches, then snagged again.

Fargo did not give up. He slipped his hands under the pole and lifted. His fingers were stung by the glacial water.

It reminded him of how frigid his feet had been a minute ago. Yet now they did not feel cold at all.

Alarm flared. Fargo knew many a trapper and prospector who had lost a finger or toe to frostbite. At such high altitude, a man's limbs froze so fast that often he did not realize it until it was too late. Once circulation was cut off, it had to be restored quickly.

Fargo rocked with more force than ever. The travois gave a grating lurch and was in the clear. He smiled as Morning Flower rode onto solid ground, then began to follow her. To his consternation, he nearly tripped over his own feet. They were sluggish to respond, and tingled terribly.

"What is wrong?" the widow wanted to know.

"Nothing," Fargo fibbed, plowing onward. He attempted to wriggle his toes and could not feel a thing. "But it would be nice if you could get a fire going." He skirted the large rock the travois had snagged on. "A small fire," he amended.

Morning Flower swung lithely from her mount, her full figure outlined against her buckskin dress. Her remarkable beauty was breathtaking, and for a few moments Fargo forgot all about his feet. He liked the way her hips swayed as she walked, and her dignified bearing. There was no denying she had an air about her. In many ways, Morning Flower was more ladylike than many a blue blood back in the States.

Fargo had ten feet to cover to reach shore. He waded as fast as he could, his calves growing more chilled with every stride. At the bank, he sank to his knees and climbed up beside the Ovaro.

The Ute woman was moving off across the meadow, gathering dead grass as she went.

Fargo tucked his right knee to his chest in order to remove his boot. It was so wet it clung to him like a second skin. Twisting and tugging, he managed to get it off. His sock was just as drenched, and he wrung it out before draping it over a small rock to dry.

Cupping his toes, Fargo massaged them. The tingling grew worse, which he took as a good sign. He slapped his foot a few times and was rewarded with a stinging sensation. It wasn't as bad as he had thought.

Reaching for his other boot, Fargo glanced up to see what had become of Morning Flower. The lovely Ute had nearly crossed the meadow. As he looked on, she faced the outcropping of earth and boulders and went as stiff as a board. Flinging the dead grass down, she spun and raced toward him.

In another moment Fargo understood why. Around the jagged ridge galloped a pair of white men. Men Fargo recognized.

They rode with Wolf Rollins.

8

So intent were the pair of gunmen on catching Morning Flower that they did not notice Skye Fargo right away. One of them glanced toward the horses but Fargo was on the ground on the far side and escaped scrutiny.

Pushing himself up, Fargo drew the Colt. He started to step around the stallion and nearly fell on his face when his numb feet refused to do as he wanted them to. Grabbing his saddle to keep from going down, he steadied himself.

Morning Flower was as fleet as a doe. Bounding gracefully across the meadow, for a few seconds she held her own. Then the horses gained on her, converging from the right and the left, the killers whooping and laughing. Their lecherous expressions left no doubt as to what they had in mind.

Fargo extended his arm over the pinto. Cocking the hammer, he aimed just as the man he was going to shoot spotted him. The gunman bellowed a warning to his companion and swerved, hunching low over the pommel of his saddle. Fargo's shot was a fraction of a second too late.

Both of Wolf's men looped around toward the ridge, firing as they fled.

Fargo had time for one more shot. He did not rush it. Sighting on the gunman who sat straightest in the saddle, he elevated the Colt to compensate for the range and stroked the trigger.

The killer jerked like a puppet that had had its strings severed. He slumped, his right arm going limp. But he stayed astride his mount and in moments he was safely past the end of the ridge and out of sight. The other one was right on his heels.

Morning Flower reached the horses. She had left her rifle leaning against the travois, and now she snatched it up and backed around the pinto to join Fargo. "I saw those men before," she disclosed, "with Wolf Rollins several sleeps ago, when he was trying to find you along the east fork of the San Jaun."

"What the hell are they doing way up here?" Fargo muttered. He searched the crown of the ridge, figuring the gunmen would go for the high ground.

"Wolf Rollins and the rest of his men might be close by," Morning Flower said. "We must get away while we still can."

She was right, of course, Fargo admitted. But the only way they could outdistance pursuit was by leaving the travois behind, and he was loath to do so. The poor woman had been through so much already. Now she stood to lose the few meager worldly goods she owned. "Cut your travois loose," he said.

While Morning Flower complied, Fargo slipped into his soaked boot. So much for a nice warm fire. He stuffed the wet sock into a saddlebag, then holstered the pistol and yanked out the Henry. The gunmen had yet to show their faces. Either the wounded one was being tended by his pard, or they were racing hell-bent for leather to fetch Wolf Rollins.

Fargo covered Morning Flower as she mounted. She did likewise for him. They left the travois lying at the edge of the creek and angled to the southwest, down toward the deep timber. It was the only real cover for miles around.

Fargo's feet hurt more the farther he rode. He could wriggle the toes on his right but not those on his left, and that bothered him some. The last thing he needed at that moment was to come down with a case of frostbite.

As if the lovely Ute could read him like a book, she asked, "Are your feet all right?"

"Fine," Fargo said a bit more gruffly than he should have.

Morning Flower took it in stride. "Men are such terrible liars. When we stop, I will take a look at them."

Fargo was about to say that he did not need anyone

mothering him, but just then he glanced toward the summit of Treasure Mountain and saw a knot of riders sweep around the ridge. The cutthroats were halfway to the creek when one of them pointed at Morning Flower and him and yelled. The entire wolf pack veered to give chase.

"Hell!" Fargo fumed, applying his spurs.

The widow had to shout to make herself heard above the drumming of their mounts. "As my Joe liked to say, some days nothing goes right."

Fargo scowled. A day or two here and there he could handle, but this was turning into the longest string of bad luck he'd ever had. Just when he thought that he finally had things under control, fate would rear up and slap him in the face.

The ground was steep and treacherous. It became even more so when they came to a stretch of talus. Fargo would much rather have gone around but there was no time to spare. He leaned back and firmed his grip on the reins as stones and loose dirt spewed out from under the Ovaro's hooves. The pinto tried to slow down but its own momentum and weight worked against it. Choking clouds of dust swirled up, making it hard for Fargo to see and harder to breathe. He coughed and blinked, his eyes watering over, blurring everything.

Morning Flower called out but Fargo could not hear what she said. The clatter and rattle of stones and earth had become a dull roar. He swiped at the dust and glimpsed trees below, but it was impossible to gauge how close they were.

A more immediate worry was the prospect of the Ovaro crashing into a large boulder. Fargo saw one flash by to his right. Seconds later another loomed in front of them. He hauled on the reins with all his might. By a miracle, the stallion missed it.

Morning Flower yelled again. Fargo wished he knew what she was saying because it was probably important. Then the faint crackle of gunfire gave him a clue. The outlaws were shooting at them! A slug whistled above his head. If the talus slope didn't get them, flying lead would.

Suddenly the Ovaro lurched forward. Fargo nearly went

flying. The dust cloud fell away, and he saw that they were on solid ground again. Ahead reared the pines. "We're almost there!" he shouted for Morning Flower's benefit, looking to his left.

She wasn't there.

Fargo snapped around.

The mare had gone down just yards from the bottom of the talus. It was on its side, thrashing wildly. Morning Flower was partially pinned and trying valiantly to free herself as slugs rained down around her.

Wolf Rollins and his men had halted at the upper edge of the debris. Rollins stood out plainly, thanks to his broad-brimmed black hat. He was one of the few not firing.

Heedless of the peril, Fargo wheeled the stallion and flew back up the slope. He banged off five shots, forcing some of the killers to scatter. At the talus, he drew rein and vaulted down. Scrambling to the mare, he gripped Morning Flower's outstretched hand and pulled. Bullets spanged off rocks on both sides of them. One struck the mare with a loud thud. The horse nickered stridently, then was still.

Morning Flower's leg slid out. Fargo hauled her to her feet, hooked his arm around her slender waist, and sped back down. Lead peppered the earth close to their feet. He sprang into the saddle, bent and swung her up, spurring into motion before she was behind him. Morning Flower clung to his shoulders, breathing heavily.

The pines closed around them. Fargo did not slow down, though. He went faster, knowing they were not yet out of rifle range.

A low limb materialized in front of them. There was no time to swerve. "Get down!" Fargo warned, ducking and tugging on Morning Flower. She pressed against him, her breasts mashing against his back. They passed under the branch with less than an inch to spare.

For the next half an hour Fargo rode like a madman, stopping only when the Ovaro was lathered with sweat and showed signs of flagging. In a small clearing screened by brush and trees, he finally reined up.

There had been no sign of the outlaws. Fargo guessed that Rollins had done the smart thing and gone around the talus slope rather than try to cross it. That would delay the killers awhile. "We can rest here a spell," he announced, "but not long."

Morning Flower slid down. Her dress hiked high on her legs, affording Fargo a tantalizing glimpse of her womanly charms. He shook himself to dispel the hunger it provoked. Now was hardly the time or the place, he told himself.

Dismounting, Fargo opened his saddlebags and rummaged for his spare set of socks. He walked a few yards and sat to strip off his boots. In all the excitement, he had forgotten about his feet. Sensation had returned to his toes but they still pained him whenever he moved. Using grass, he wiped his feet dry, then slid on the woolen socks.

With a sigh, Morning Flower sat next to him. "Thank you for saving my life. We are even now."

"I'm sorry about your mare," Fargo said.

"She was a good animal," Morning Flower stated. "She never gave me any cause to complain."

Fargo tugged his boots on. They were still damp inside and had to be forced. He started to lean back to rest, then remembered the shots he had fired.

The rule of thumb for any frontiersman was to always reload as soon as possible. Fargo replaced the spent cartridges in his Colt first, then reached into a pocket for a .44 cartridge for the Henry.

Loading the rifle took more effort. Fargo had to press a thumb lug at the end of the tubular magazine. It, in turn, compressed a spring that worked the lug up or down an open slot running the length of the magazine. One by one he inserted five rounds. He inspected the slot to be sure no dirt had collected in it and blew on some dust near the top. It wouldn't do to have the Henry foul when he needed it most.

Morning Flower watched him. "I am afraid I lost the Sharps when my mare went down," she remarked. "I will not be of much use if those wicked men catch up with us."

Fargo recalled that the rifle had belonged to her husband. "Once we shake Wolf and his friends, we'll circle around and see if we can find it."

"That would be too dangerous."

"It has sentimental value, doesn't it?"

She looked at him. "Why are you doing all this for me, Skye Fargo? Until three sleeps ago, we did not even know one another."

"That should make a difference?"

Morning Flower's rose petal lips compressed. "No," she said thoughtfully. "It should not." Slowly, almost fearfully, she leaned toward him.

Fargo was taken by surprise. Her soft mouth covered his and he felt her lips part. The silken tip of her tongue rubbed against his teeth, then entwined with his tongue in a languid, gliding caress that sparked a twitch below his belt. Her dusky scent was bewitching.

It was the sort of kiss two young lovers might share, and Morning Flower let it go on and on. Fargo stroked her arm. He desired to do a lot more, but under the circumstances he put a cap on his boiling passion. When she pulled back, the taste of her lingered in his mouth. It brought to mind honey and wine and everything fine.

Morning Flower lowered her head. "I should not have done that."

"Did you hear me complain?"

"My Joe would never forgive me."

Fargo gently took hold of her chin and raised it so he could see her face. Moisture glistened in her eyes. He chose his next words with care. "Your Joe has been gone quite some time. It's nice that you honor his memory, but from what you've told me about him, I doubt he would want you to live the rest of your life all alone. You have to let go. You have to learn to live again."

Her voice was that of a ten-year-old deathly terrified of the dark. "It is very hard."

"No one ever claimed life would be easy." Fargo pecked her on the cheek, then stood. As much as he would have liked to take her into his arms and caress her from head to toe, he had Wolf Rollins to think of. "We'd better head out," he suggested.

The Ovaro had its second wind. Fargo continued to the southwest for several miles. From the crest of a switchback he surveyed the higher slopes and saw no trace of the hardcases. It troubled him. Wolf Rollins did not impress him as the kind of man who would just give up. So where were they?

Toward the middle of the afternoon, Fargo looped to the west. He had not gone far when he emerged from the trees onto a grassy slope and spied a gurgling stream below.

"Fall Creek, your people call it," Morning Flower informed him. "Lower down is a waterfall."

Fargo was more interested in a shaded pool he could see. Nudging the Ovaro down the incline, he halted at the water's edge. A butterfly fluttered by. A beetle cleaved the surface of the creek. Something flashed along the bottom, a fish, perhaps. "This is as good a place as any to spend the night," he proposed. "You rest while I unsaddle my horse."

Morning Flower was sliding off. "It would not be fair to leave all the work for you." Scouring the clearing, she located several sizeable stones. "I will not be gone long," she said, and flitted off into the undergrowth.

Fargo let her go. She needed to keep busy, to take her mind off all she had been through. Stripping the Ovaro, he placed his saddle at the base of a towering fir, then spread out his bedroll. In short order he had a small fire going. As he intended, the tendrils of smoke were dissipated by the limbs overhead. There was little likelihood of anyone spotting it from a distance.

Shucking his boots and socks, Fargo leaned against the saddle and placed his feet close to the flames. The warmth felt wonderful. His right foot had stopped bothering him but not his left. It was numb at the top, and his two smallest toes were unnaturally white.

Given time, Fargo was confident he would mend. He had been lucky. It was an extremely mild case of frostbite, brought on more by the icy water freezing his already sweaty feet than the cold water alone. If the water temperature had been five or ten degrees lower, it would have cost him dearly.

Fargo gazed toward the summit, rimmed by its thin mantle of snow. He wondered if Wolf Rollins was still up there, and whether the Utes were still on his trail. Not to mention

Ike McDermott. It seemed as if every time he turned around, someone else was out for his blood.

His first priority, Fargo decided, was to get Morning Flower to safety. But where could he take her? Certainly not back to her people, since Tall Bear would never give her a moment's peace. And certainly not to Pagosa Springs or whatever the fledgling town was calling itself, since most whites regarded the Utes as bitter enemies. Her one friend, the prospector, had proven to be shy a few marbles.

Where else was left?

Fargo closed his eyes to rest a few moments, and before he knew it, he dozed. It could not have been long after when the rustle of someone approaching through the brush brought him wide awake in a flash. Raising the Henry, he swiveled.

"Do not shoot. It is I."

Morning Flower carried a bloody rabbit. Sitting across from him, she drew her knife. "My Joe liked to say that no one else was as skilled at bringing one of these down with a rock as I am. But then he always praised me when it was not called for."

Fargo merely smiled. She appeared to be in much better spirits than she had been when she left, and he did not want to say or do anything that would spoil her mood.

"Do you like rabbit meat?"

"One of my favorites," Fargo admitted.

Morning Flower nodded. "I thought so. You are a lot like my Joe inside as well as outside." Deftly wielding the blade, she lopped off the head, then turned the rabbit over to skin it. "Are you by any chance looking for a woman to live with?"

Fargo had almost forgotten how frank Indian women could be. Unlike their white sisters, they didn't beat around the bush when they had something important on their minds. "Not at this time," he answered honestly.

Fleeting disappointment showed. Then Morning Flower jabbed the knife into the rabbit, saying, "I expected you to say so, but it did not hurt to ask. One day I hope to find another man like my Joe." She glanced at him. "I will make him the happiest man alive."

"I don't doubt it," Fargo assured her. And he meant every word. She was the type of woman any sensible man would give his eyeteeth to go through life with. So what did that say about him?

"Until that day," Morning Flower had gone on, "I will take your advice. I will not live in the past so much."

They made small talk while she carved up their supper. She told about her childhood among the Utes, he talked about a few of the many interesting places he had visited. When she learned that he had seen the Pacific Ocean, she badgered him with questions. It was a lifelong dream of hers to see the Great Water one day.

Going into the forest, Morning Flower brought back two forked branches and a slender straight limb she trimmed of bark and leaves. Soon dripping morsels of succulent rabbit hung on a spit over the fire, roasting slowly as she turned the limb.

Fargo had not realized how famished he was until he caught a whiff of the delicious aroma. Rousing himself, he took his coffee pot to the stream, filled it, and added Arbuckle's.

The forest was tranquil. It was the quiet hour before the sun went down, when the animals that were abroad during the day sought their dens and burrows and nests, and the animals that were abroad after dark started to come to life after a full day's rest. Few birds sang. Even the wind had died down.

Morning Flower lifted the spit to inspect the meat. "Supper is ready," she declared, and pried off a piece for him to taste.

Fargo knew Indian customs well. He ate with relish, smacking his lips often and giving a grunt of contentment when he was done. "I may not be in the market for a woman, but my stomach is in love."

The widow was pleased. She had brought back two long flat sections of bark, and now she covered one with meat and gave it to him. "Eat your fill. There is plenty left for me."

As Fargo accepted it, their fingers brushed. He nearly jumped as an electric shock rippled up his arm.

Morning Flower gasped and recoiled as if burned. She held her hand up, glanced at him, and laughed. "That has only happened to me once before. The first time I touched my Joe."

In silence they finished their meal. Fargo left enough rabbit to serve as a meager breakfast. He savored three brimming cups of coffee and was pouring a fourth when distant sounds wafted to their ears from high up Treasure Mountain. There were four evenly spaced shots, then a flurry of gunfire, rifles, and pistols mixed.

"What does it mean?" Morning Flower mused.

"Maybe Wolf Rollins ran into Tall Bear," Fargo speculated. He thought that he heard the deep boom of a Sharps in the din, and remembered that Ike McDermott owned one.

A minute later the firing ceased.

Fargo set down his cup. His socks and boots were long since dry, so he put them on, grabbed the Henry, and walked to the top of the nearby slope. Whoever was up there might venture lower, and he wanted to be ready for them.

The sun had just dipped below the horizon, but already lengthening shadows were gobbling up what little light remained. Fargo watched and listened until it was so dark that he couldn't see the tops of the closest trees.

Fairly sure that they would be safe until morning, Fargo went back down. Their fire had burned low. The bark plates had been disposed of, and the coffee pot had been put to one side. The Ute woman was nowhere to be seen.

"Morning Flower?" Fargo called softly. A splash drew his attention to the pool. Lying on the bank was her long beaded dress. He stepped to the edge and saw a tawny form knife under the water toward him. Thinking that she might prefer some privacy, he went to step back.

Morning Flower broke the surface as smoothly as a water nymph. She made no attempt to cover herself, but stood there with glistening beads running down her lush body. Her braids had been undone, allowing her raven hair to hang well past her shoulders.

Fargo watched a particular drop fall from the tip of her

oval chin onto her chest, and from there flow between her exquisite breasts. Her nipples were hard and peaked, her stomach as flat as a board. The swell of her bronzed thighs was enticing beyond belief.

"Would you care for a swim?" she asked huskily. "The water is pleasant."

Fargo's throat was as dry as a desert. He had to swallow twice before he could reply. "I'd like that very much." Placing the Henry on top of her dress, he slowly stripped to the buff.

Morning Flower did not move. Her eyes devoured him as he straightened and stepped into the pool.

The water was not quite as cold as the runoff in Treasure Creek, but it was frigid enough to cause Fargo's left foot to throb. Goose bumps broke out all over him. He stopped to let his body adjust, and Morning Flower advanced, halting when her nipples were about to rub against him. He looked at them and felt himself growing warm all over. There was no mistaking her intentions. "You claimed that you wanted to swim," he reminded her.

"I lied."

Their bodies joined.

9

Skye Fargo had learned long ago that there was no telling how women would act from one moment to the next. They were as unpredictable as tornados, as temperamental as mustangs. Fire one minute, ice the next. Sugar and spice one day, hell on two legs the day after.

Based on the way Morning Flower had acted since they met, Fargo fully expected she would be shy about exposing her luscious figure, yet she had brazenly stood up right in front of him, naked to the world.

And given how reserved the widow always was, how prim and proper she carried herself, Fargo had figured she would also shy away from an intimate embrace. Yet when their bodies molded together in the pool, it was as if he embraced a living, breathing inferno of raw, unchecked lust.

Morning Flower seized him by the hair, pulled his face down to hers, and mashed her full lips against his with an urgency that was almost painful. From deep within her issued a low animal moan as her tongue speared between his parted lips and wrestled his against the roof of his mouth. At the same time she ground herself into him, her crinkly thatch brushing his stiff pole as her thighs caressed his.

Fargo was going to tell her to take it slow, that they had all the time in the world, but she never broke for air. Her mouth was glued to his. Her tongue would not leave his alone. She breathed through her nostrils, loudly, lustily, panting more and more as her arousal peaked.

Morning Flower dug her nails into his shoulders, lightly at first, but deeper as the moments passed. When he reached around to cup her firm buttocks, she moaned louder and slowly raked her fingers down his back on either side of his spine. She grasped his behind and squeezed his cheeks, kneading them as if they were so much dough. Her knee slid between his legs to stroke up and down.

Heady desire more potent than any wine intoxicated Fargo. He wanted her with every fiber of his being. He craved to plunge into her, to hear her cry out, to make her shudder with release. It took great force of will not to rush things, not to turn and throw her onto the bank and consummate their union before it had really begun.

Morning Flower let go of Fargo's bottom. For a moment her hands were not touching him and he idly wondered what she was doing with them. Then he found out. Hot fingers closed on his manhood. Others cupped his engorged oysters and delicately massaged them.

It was almost too much. Fargo nearly exploded. The sensation was stimulating beyond belief. He stiffened and gasped and felt rather than saw her lips curl in a smile even as she kept on kissing him. It reminded him that despite her coy behavior at times, she was a hot-blooded woman who knew what she wanted and had no qualms about getting it.

They had that in common. Fargo now covered her rock hard nipples and gently squeezed. It was as if a lightning bolt seared her from head to toe. She arced her back, tossed her head, and called out softly in the Ute tongue. Fargo had no way of knowing what she said, but he did not need to understand the words to divine their meaning. She was in ecstasy.

Fargo tweaked the nipples, not hard enough to cause discomfort but still hard enough to elicit a rumbling groan and to have her rub her legs together as if she were trying to set herself afire. Her nipples were supremely sensitive, so big and full they were like flower petals in full bloom. Smothering one with his mouth, he almost lost his balance when Morning Flower thrust against him and clung to him, quivering uncontrollably.

Fargo's left foot was throbbing but he hardly noticed. Sheer sensual hunger dominated him. He switched his mouth to her other breast, lathering it as he had the first.

Morning Flower wasn't idle either. Her knowing fingers had his organ pulsing from tip to stem. His swollen rocks were hard enough to shatter steel. She also slipped a hand between his legs and lightly ran her fingers back and forth.

Dropping a hand to her legs, Fargo rubbed her inner thighs from her knees to her thatch. She opened her legs wider to permit entry and he obliged her by sliding his right hand between them. His thumb brushed the tiny knob at her core and she cried out, a yip of feral pleasure such as the very first woman must have uttered when mating with the very first man. The cry became a strangled moan when Fargo pried her nether lips apart and inserted a forefinger part of the way into her slick tunnel. Her breath caught in her throat. Her breasts heaved.

Fargo held still until she quieted. Then he probed deeper, a fraction at a time. Her sheath closed around his finger and seemed to try to draw it all the way inside herself, but he dallied, for her benefit more than his, swirling his finger to increase the delicious friction that was sending ripples of indescribable rapture through her.

At last Morning Flower spoke in English. "Ohhhhhh, yes, handsome one. You make me feel just like my Joe did. You make me feel—" Her statement was choked off by a racking sob as Fargo suddenly jammed his finger in to the knuckle. She trembled, her lips a perfect circle, her eyes wide but unfocused.

Fargo pumped, lightly to begin, setting the tempo for what was to come. Her vibrant body automatically adjusted to the rhythm. It was as if he were tuning a musical instrument for the right tone and pitch. Her mouth swooped to his throat and she nibbled on his soft flesh, pinpricks all the more arousing because at the same time her warm breath was blowing on his skin.

When Fargo judged the time to be right, he inserted a second finger. Her womanhood throbbed. His thumb found the tiny knob and pressed ever so gently. She closed her legs around his arm and pushed her crack against it. A throaty growl greeted a stab of his fingers.

For a while Fargo gave her luscious globes attention. His mouth drifted higher and she locked hers on his. To Fargo, she had the taste of warmed-over honey, so sweet, so sugary, that he could not get enough of it. Strands of her hair swirled around his broad shoulders and one of her hands rose to the small of his back to trace small circles.

Suddenly pulling back, Morning Flower declared, "I am ready! Please! Now!"

Fargo put his hands under her arms and hoisted her off her feet. She did not weigh all that much, so it was easy for him to position her above his manhood and slowly ease her lower. Morning Flower helped by slipping a hand down and holding his organ steady until the tip of his member slid into her. Fargo paused. Their eyes met. He smiled, and impaled her.

Morning Flower shrieked. She thrashed. Her scabbard enfolded his sword as if the two were made for one another. Blowing through her nose, she gulped and said, "So big! So hard!"

Carefully easing her back until she floated from the waist up, Fargo reveled in the sight of her golden form, in the upturned peaks crowning her breasts, in the smooth muscles covering her abdomen. She was all any man could ever ask for, more than most would ever know. He molded her breasts into twin pyramids while she bucked her bottom into him. The water splashed up over her stomach, but no higher.

Planting his feet solidly, Fargo gripped her by the shoulders. His initial thrust caused her to churn the creek with her flailing legs and arms. His next induced her to wrap her legs around him. She smiled languidly, her eyes lambent pools.

"It has been so long! So very long!"

There was no need to ask what she meant. Fargo continued to plunge into her. He slid one hand down to her hip and clamped fast so she would not slip off his rigid pole. The water was better than a mattress, her buoyant body responding as if she were afloat on a layer of air. She grasped his arms and bucked against him, her fervor the equal of his.

Fargo closed his eyes and relished the gradually building tingle deep in his loins. The soft slap of water against his hips and buttocks added to his pleasure. For a while he could forget all about the outlaws and the Utes and the treacherous prospector. For a while he could totally relax and give himself up to the moment at hand.

Harder and harder Fargo pumped. Harder and harder Morning Flower met his thrusts. The slap of their bodies grew louder, as did the slap of water against the two of them and against the bank. It sounded as if a storm were rising, its wind whipping the surface into waves.

In truth, there was a storm building. Two brewing storms of elemental passion, inside Fargo and the widow. They pounded one another, eager for mutual release but not eager to reach the pinnacle too soon. Like a pair of thoroughbreds pacing each other, so they matched one another in the intensity of their coupling.

Fargo was determined that she would go over the brink before he did. When his manhood was on the verge of bursting, he clenched his teeth and held the explosion in. He thought of anything and everything that might distract him, such as the stars and the trees and the pool. When that failed, he mentally roared at himself to hold it in just a little while longer. A few more minutes was all it should take.

Actually, less. Morning Flower gasped, dug her nails into him, and half rose out of the water. She gave him the most peculiar look. Then her eyelids fluttered and she sank back. For a few seconds she was as still as a log.

Fargo wondered if she had passed out. Slowing, he leaned forward to check on her when suddenly she shrieked and let herself go wild with abandon. She became a whirlwind, almost impossible to hold, scream after scream tearing from her throat. It occurred to Fargo that she was making enough noise to be heard a mile away, but he didn't care. He wasn't about to stop.

Morning Flower gushed. It triggered Fargo's own pent up urge. The night seemed to thunder to the pounding of his temples. He could not help groaning. Rocking on the balls of his feet, he slammed into her until they were both spent. She was first to go limp. He had to catch her to keep her from going under. Bracing her shoulders, he moved to shore and placed her on the grass. She mumbled something as he sprawled out next to her, draping an arm across her chest.

"I didn't quite hear that," Fargo said.

"Thank you, Joe, my love."

Fargo glanced at her. She had slipped into dreamland and was probably not aware of what she was saying. Caressing her cheek, he rested his chin on her shoulder and let himself drift off.

It was not Fargo's intention to sleep long but his body could not be denied. So sound was his slumber that it shocked him to wake up on hearing the Ovaro nicker and discover that dawn was less than an hour off. Their fire had long since gone out.

The big stallion was staring into the inky forest on the other side of the pool. Whether man or beast had alarmed it was irrelevant. Odds were, whoever or whatever was out there would not be friendly.

Fargo stepped to the Henry. Bare-assed, he crouched close to the saddle and scanned the foliage. Did something move, or were his eyes deceiving him? He leveled the rifle but had nothing to shoot.

After a while the pinto lost interest and cropped at the grass. Fargo figured that whatever had been there was gone. Dressing, he strapped on the Colt and donned his hat. Thanks to a few burning embers he rekindled the fire in no time but did not let the flames shoot very high.

Presently coffee was perking. Fargo treated himself to a cup, roving his gaze again and again over the widow's sultry form. She was something special. If he had been of a mind to dig in roots, he could do a hell of a lot worse. Somehow, he had to help her out of the fix she was in. It was the least he could do.

Fargo let her sleep until a golden crown rimmed the far eastern horizon. Taking her dress, he hunkered down and gently shook her shoulder.

"Joe?" Morning Flower said dreamily, then opened her eyes. "Oh! It's you!" she blurted, sitting up. "My goodness. Did I sleep the night away? Why didn't you wake me? I would have stood guard if you asked."

"Don't feel bad. I haven't been up all that long myself." Fargo gave her the dress. "I'll heat up what's left of the rabbit meat while you tend to whatever it is that women do in the morning."

Morning Flower clasped his hand as he turned. "I want to thank you for last night. It was wonderful. I have not been with a man since—"

"There's no call for you to explain yourself," Fargo interrupted. "We did what we did because we both wanted to. I'm just grateful you picked me."

The widow abruptly seemed to realize she was naked. Holding the dress in front of her, she rose and scooted backward into the brush.

Fargo chuckled as he ambled to the spit. He didn't know what it was about some women. They'd lie at a man's side from dusk until dawn without a stitch of clothing on, but once the sun came up, off they'd rush to cover themselves. It wasn't as if the man was going to see anything he hadn't already seen and fondled to his heart's content. Yet woman after woman did the same thing.

Morning Flower returned as Fargo lifted the meat from the fire. He had already poured a cup of coffee for her, and now set a piece of rabbit on a flat stone beside it. "Breakfast is served," he announced.

The beautiful Ute woman knelt and raised the tin cup. "I have been thinking." She swallowed a few times. "It is not right that I be a burden to you. If we can find my rifle, I will go my own way."

Fargo was not about to abandon her when she needed a friend the most, but to humor her he asked, "Go where? Anywhere you turn, you have enemies waiting to do you in."

"Five sleeps north of Treasure Mountain live another band of my people. I have cousins there. Maybe one of them will take me in."

"Maybe," Fargo stressed.

"As you made clear last night, it is time I got on with my life. It is time I put Joe behind me." Morning Flower swirled the coffee in her cup. "I am still young. I can cook, I can sew, I know how to keep a knife sharp. There is bound to be a warrior who will think me worthy to share his lodge."

That was an understatement. The way Fargo saw it, every unmarried male in the village would be courting her within a few days of her arrival. "If that's what you really want, I'll take you there."

"It would not be safe. They like whites even less than the people in my own village."

"I don't care. I'm not letting you out of my sight until I'm sure you'll be safe," Fargo said flatly.

"As you wish," Morning Flower said, sounding immensely pleased by his concern.

They finished their breakfast. Fargo saddled the Ovaro, forked leather, and helped her up behind him. As the sun climbed, so did they, looping to the west for a few more miles before changing to due north and eventually to an easterly bearing that brought them to the vicinity of the talus slope shortly after noon.

Fargo rode with one hand on the butt of his Colt. He drew rein on coming out of a stand of spruce and discovering day-old tracks made by shod horses. The exact number was difficult to judge. "Wolf Rollins and his friends," he remarked. "Heading southwest."

"Hunting for us," Morning Flower said.

"Let them." Fargo clucked the pinto forward. "We'll be long gone before they figure out what we did."

Three circling buzzards guided them to the exact spot. Three more were feasting on the mare. One had just pecked out an eyeball. It gave a convulsive gulp as they halted, then hissed like an angry serpent. The other two waddled away. So graceful in the air, on the ground they were as ungainly as drunken sailors.

"Ugly creatures," Morning Flower said.

Fargo wasn't all that fond of them himself, but he wouldn't go that far. Vultures had their purpose in the greater scheme of things. Without scavengers, the flesh of dead animals would be left to fester and rot and stink up the landscape, to say nothing of the diseases that might be spread. He got down and walked straight toward the stubborn cuss on the mare. It held its ground for all of five seconds, then broke into a lumbering trot, spread its long wings, and flapped upward. The other pair were quick to join the exodus.

Fargo scoured the immediate area but did not see the rifle. "Were you still holding on to the Sharps when your horse went down?" he asked.

Morning Flower reflected. "I believe I was. It all happened so fast." She studied the slope above. "I remember my mare almost fell several times, but I had the rifle in my left hand until the very end."

"Is that so?" Fargo said, an idea leading his steps to the mare. He circled it slowly, playing out his hunch. A few inches behind the saddle he found what he was looking for. "I'll need your help," he said.

The widow picked her way up the talus with care. When she saw the tip of the rifle barrel jutting out from under the dead animal, she smiled. "I never would have guessed."

Squatting, Fargo slid his hand under the mare on either side of the Sharps. "This might be a waste of our time. For all we know, the stock is busted to pieces." He nodded at the barrel. "When I lift, pull as hard as you can."

Morning Flower was skeptical. "No man can pick up an entire horse. Not even you."

"It's just this part we have to worry about," Fargo said, touching the hide above the rifle with his knee. "Now get set." Waiting until she gripped the muzzle with both hands, he coiled his legs, heaved upward, and barked, "Now!"

It was like trying to raise a ten-ton boulder. The mare was so much dead weight, and Fargo had to exert every sinew in his powerful frame to even budge it. A fraction at a time, the animal's back rose. Not high. Not more than half an inch. And that was as high as he could manage.

The widow lurched backwards, her heels scrabbling for solid footing, and the Sharps began to slide out from under the horse.

"Don't stop!" Fargo rasped, well aware he was red in the face and that every vein on his neck and temples bulged. He sputtered. He felt his grip slipping. "Hurry!"

Morning Flower had pulled the barrel out far enough to expose the rear sight. She tugged and tugged but it was caught and would not budge any more. Giving a yell, she thrust herself backwards. The rifle jerked, then popped free, catching her by surprise and throwing her onto her backside. "We did it!"

Fargo stepped back, breathing deeply. He took the Sharps and examined it. All his effort had not been in vain. The stock was badly scraped and nicked and a rock had gouged a groove in the wooden forearm, but otherwise the rifle was in perfect working order. "Your luck has taken a turn for the better," he commented.

"It took a turn for the better last night," Morning Flower said, the look on her face leaving no doubt as to her meaning. Accepting the rifle, she worked the trigger guard, lowering the breechblock to expose the cartridge still in the chamber. "It works just like it should," she said happily.

Fargo thought of his old Sharps, and how he had given it up for the newer Henry. As powerful as a .52-caliber Sharps was, even the best of shooters could only fire one four or five times a minute. That did not even begin to compare to the Henry's rate of close to thirty rounds in the same amount of time.

It had been hard for Fargo to stop using his old Sharps, which had seen him safely through many a shooting scrape, but he would have been a fool not to take advantage of a rifle that let its user load on Sunday and shoot all week, as the saying went.

"Now for the travois," Fargo said, heading for the Ovaro.

"Has your stallion ever pulled one before?" Morning Flower inquired.

"No. But there's a first time for everything." Fargo climbed on his horse. "Besides, all we have to do is get it down the mountain into the heavy timber. We'll cache your belongings until you can come back for them."

The ride up took much longer than had the ride down. Carrying the two of them up one steep slope after another sapped even the Ovaro's reservoir of strength. Fargo stopped so the pinto could rest twice before they passed the last of the pines. Soon the low ridge flanked by the meadow appeared. Fargo angled toward the bank of Treasure Creek, where they had left the travois.

"Look!" Morning Flower suddenly exclaimed, pointing. "Someone has moved it!"

Clear across the meadow, at the bottom of the ridge, was the travois. It had been propped against a boulder, but other than that it appeared to be intact. All her possessions were lashed to the platform, just as they had been.

Fargo promptly stopped. Something did not sit right. Who, he wondered, would have gone to all the trouble of toting the travois way over there, then just left it? He stayed where he was a while, looking and listening, suspicious of a trap.

"Why do you delay?" Morning Flower asked. "I am sure Wolf Rollins must be to blame. When he saw there was nothing of value, he went his way."

It was as good an explanation as any. Fargo went on at a walk, studying the ridge. As he drew rein near the travois, he observed plenty of tracks, but they had been made by *unshod* horses. He halted a second time.

Just as a swarm of Utes descended on them.

10

The only reason Skye Fargo did not die on the spot was that the Utes wanted to take him alive. Yipping and screeching, they swept down the ridge, none other than Tall Bear in the lead. There were at least thirty, maybe more. Fargo couldn't tell. And he didn't linger to count them.

The instant the war party materialized, Fargo wheeled the Ovaro and streaked off across the meadow. He nearly lost Morning Flower, who had started to dismount and had to clutch at him to keep from toppling off. Whipping the reins and using his spurs, Fargo spurred the stallion into a burst of speed that gained them a dozen yards in half as many seconds.

The Utes fanned out, still hollering, many wearing smiles. They believed that Fargo and the woman were as good as caught. They were the cats; Fargo and Morning Flower the mice. To them, the pursuit was a grand game with a foregone conclusion.

Fortunately, Fargo had an ace in the hole. The Utes had no idea how fast the Ovaro was, or any notion of the stallion's tremendous stamina. Fargo hoped they wouldn't realize the truth until it was too late.

The pinto hit the slope on the fly, a blur of black and white. Fargo bent low over the saddle horn to better distribute his weight and avoid throwing the stallion off stride. Morning Flower took his cue and bent low against him.

Mere moments later the tenor of the shouts and howls changed. From those of ribald mirth, the Utes' cries took on a tone of baffled outrage.

Fargo lashed the reins harder. He glanced back, noting which Utes were the fleetest, the ones who posed the most threat. Tall Bear was one of them but he was no longer in the lead.

The timber line seemed impossibly far off, yet it was their only hope. Eventually the Utes would think to pick them off. They had to gain cover.

The thought no sooner crossed Fargo's mind than he heard Tall Bear bellowing above the din. It sounded as if the warrior were giving specific commands to the others. He twisted to ask Morning Flower what the tall Ute had said but she beat him to the punch.

"Tall Bear just told the rest to shoot your horse! He is afraid we will get away if they do not!"

So far Fargo had held off from firing in the belief that if he did not slay any of them, they would go on treating the chase as a lark. That now changed. Palming the Colt, he shifted as several rifles cracked. In swift succession he banged off three shots, and at each blast one of the nearest Utes threw up his arms and keeled from his mount. The others who were close immediately slowed or veered aside.

Tall Bear was enraged. His roars rang out like those of a grizzly who had been shot in the gut.

"He is offering five of his best horses to the warrior who brings us down!" Morning Flower translated.

Fargo looked back. Tall Bear was the one who wanted to get his hands on Morning Flower, and Tall Bear was the one who led the war party. If he could kill the tall warrior, the others might take that as a sign—as bad medicine—and give up. Taking deliberate aim, he fired.

A rut spoiled the shot. At the very moment Fargo stroked the trigger, the Ovaro came on the rut and stumbled. The stallion recovered instantly, flying onward, but the harm had been done. Fargo's shot missed Tall Bear and hit Tall Bear's mount instead.

The animal threw up its head, whinnied stridently, and buckled, its front legs bending first, sending it into a forward roll. Tall Bear flung himself off its bare back to keep from being crushed. He landed on his shoulder, rolled eight or nine times, and came to rest in a swirl of dust, unmoving.

A full third of the warriors rushed to his aid. Fargo hoped

that the spill had done the job but Tall Bear stirred as four warriors jumped down and sat him up.

One shot remained in the Colt. Fargo saved it for an emergency. Devoting his full attention to escaping, he fled lower, picking a course that avoided rough ground and boulders and would bring them to the timber well to the east of the talus slope. He was not about to make the same mistake twice.

The twenty or so Utes still in pursuit did not press him quite as hard as before. They had learned their lesson and were unwilling to challenge his marksmanship. Spread out over a hundred yards in a half-moon formation, they were content to stay just out of effective pistol range.

Their strategy was transparent. Fargo knew they were going to hold back until the Ovaro tired, then close in. So long as they kept the stallion in sight at all times, it wouldn't matter if Fargo reached the high timber. They would keep on following at a safe distance, always there, waiting their chance.

Fargo let them do as they pleased for the time being. He could not shake them anyway until he was among the trees. Slowing so as not to run the Ovaro into the ground before they got there, he took advantage of the lull to reload the Colt. Never easy to do at a gallop, he lost a cartridge when the stallion turned sharply to skirt a wide hole that had been formed by erosion. The abrupt movement jarred the cartridge from his fingers. He tried to catch it, but missed.

It was a full five minutes before Tall Bear and the rest of the war party caught up. Tall Bear rode double with another man, and based on the vigor with which he shook a fist at Fargo and the vehemence in his upraised voice, he was no worse the wear for the tumble he had taken.

Suddenly a young warrior off on the left, perhaps eager to collect the five horses Tall Bear had offered, came straight for the Ovaro. Armed with a lance, he slid onto the side of his sorrel. The other Utes cheered on his act of bravery by howling and waving their weapons overhead.

Fargo dared not let the young warrior get close enough to fling the lance. At close range, a lance could do much more damage than a bullet, shearing through flesh and vital organs like a hot knife through butter.

Lacking a clear target, Fargo sighted on the sorrel. He touched his finger to the trigger, then hesitated. The young Ute had his left forearm hooked over the sorrel's neck while his left heel clung to its back. Plainly visible was the warrior's left elbow. It even jutted a few inches above the horse. Grinning, Fargo fixed a bead, steadied his arm as best he could, and fired.

The elbow exploded in a shower of skin, bone, and gore, splattering blood over the sorrel. The young warrior cried out as he plummeted. The sorrel's pounding hooves missed him but he slammed headfirst into a large rock. Blood pouring down his face and arm, he tried to sit up but swayed and pitched forward. Six fellow braves raced to his side.

Fargo was confident none of the other warriors would be as foolhardy, but he did not take his eyes off them for more than a second or two at a time. All the yipping and hollering ceased. To a man, the Utes were deadly serious now. They had fallen companions to avenge, their honor to uphold. When they closed in, they would be coming in for the kill.

The tree line loomed nearer. Fargo spotted a break, an opening between pines, and made for it. The Ovaro had another twenty yards to cover when, at a shout from Tall Bear, the Utes opened up fire with a vengeance. All those with rifles used them.

Fargo had to guide the pinto and could not return their fire. He was gratified to hear Morning Flower's Sharps boom. It thundered again as they reached the timber. In a flash they were among the many trunks and clusters of brush, and Fargo called on all his riding skill to put as much distance behind him as he could before the Utes reached the vegetation.

The Ovaro was tired but game. Fargo made a point of going around logs instead of vaulting them and avoiding thickets rather than plowing through. He needed the stallion to cover a lot of ground yet.

It was not long before a belt of tall firs shaded them on

either side. Fargo could hear the crunch of many hooves and the crackle of undergrowth well to the rear. The Utes called back and forth to one another, which he took as a sign that they had lost sight of the pinto. Just as he wanted.

At the bottom of a short slope Fargo rode out onto a meadow too wide to go around. Legs slapping the Ovaro's slick hide, he raced toward more firs on the other side. They were almost there when a harsh shout rang through the air.

The Utes had spied them. The chase was on again.

Worse, the Ovaro was growing winded.

Fargo glanced back at Morning Flower. "It's no good," he told her. "We'll have to make a stand."

"Do as you think best. I will be honored to die with you fighting next to me."

Fargo was flattered, but he wasn't about to become buzzard bait if he could help it. He scanned the forest for a good place to stop. The terrain was too flat, and except for the firs offered scant cover. There had to be somewhere better.

There was. Another forty yards brought them to the brink of a shallow gully. The Ovaro automatically slowed, and Fargo hauled on the reins as they slid to the bottom.

"This has to do!" Fargo let the widow know as he leaped from the saddle. Yanking on the Henry, he dashed to the top, sank onto his left knee, and pressed the polished stock to his shoulder.

The Utes were crashing through the woods in a ragged line. At the center was a husky warrior who held a stout bow. The first to see Fargo, he called out to his friends, snapping the bow up to shoot. He was pulling back the sinew string when the Henry blasted and down he went, a new hole between his eyes.

Fargo swiveled, tracked a second rider, and fired. He did not wait to see if the man fell but shifted to fix a hasty mark on a third Ute. The Henry punched against him as lead and smoke belched from the muzzle.

Under the withering fire the Utes scattered, breaking right and left. Two more were down before the majority jumped from their horses to seek shelter behind trees and boulders and whatever else was handy. Those with rifles employed them, those with bows unleashed glittering shafts. The few who had only lances began to sneak close enough to hurl them.

Fargo stood his ground. Working the lever furiously, he blistered the forest with shots, pinning the Utes down and wounding one who showed himself. The magazine went empty. Fargo ducked below the rim to reload.

Morning Flower was gaping at the Henry in astonishment. "I have never seen a gun like yours!" she declared. "How can it shoot so many times?"

"I'll show you later, if we live long enough," Fargo responded, jerking a finger at the rim. "Do what you can to hold them back."

"Oh. Yes. Sorry." She scrambled to the top, peeked over the edge, and fired so fast that Fargo was sure she had missed until a yelp of pure agony proved otherwise. She noticed he was watching. "Joe taught me," she said proudly. "He believed I should know how to protect myself."

Fargo finished reloading, his fingers flying. He had never inserted cartridges so fast before, but he had practiced so many times that he had the Henry reloaded in about half the time it would have taken him to reload the Sharps. He straightened beside Morning Flower, glimpsed a dusky form streaking through high weeds, and felled it with a well-placed round.

Slugs kicked up puffs of dirt around them. Arrows rained down, some smacking into the earth uncomfortably close.

A bowman who rashly exposed himself to take better aim was the next to fall.

"We are holding our own!" Morning Flower declared.

But for how long? Fargo mused. The edge the Henry gave them would not keep the Utes at bay forever. "Mount up," he told her. "Be ready to ride like hell."

The widow didn't debate the point. She dutifully slid down, sticking a cartridge in the Sharps as she stood.

Fargo fired twice at random targets. Most of the Utes were stealthily converging, moving from cover to cover. Their mounts had been left well to the rear and quite a few had drifted off, spooked by the gunfire and war whoops. By leaving their horses unattended, the Utes had made a critical blunder.

Squeezing off another shot, Fargo twisted to descend. He was not quite to the bottom when Morning Flower screeched his name. A shadow fell across him. Springing from the rim was a burly Ute, tomahawk in hand. Somehow the warrior had reached the gully without being seen. Fargo brought up the Henry but the Ute was on him before he could fire. It felt as if a fallen redwood crashed down on him. The tomahawk missed his face by the width of a whisker.

Fargo slammed the Henry's stock into the man's gut, reversed his grip, and drove the barrel into the Ute's forehead. The warrior, on his knees, teetered. He swung but Fargo blocked the blow.

The gully rocked to the blast of the Big Fifty. In a scarlet spray, the lower half of the Ute's jaw disappeared. Shuddering convulsively, the warrior collapsed facedown.

Fargo pushed himself to his feet and dashed to the Ovaro, brushing a bloody tooth from his shirt. Morning Flower moved back to give him room to mount. As he did, he said over a shoulder, "Saving my hide is becoming a habit with you, isn't it?"

Gruff shouts to the north impelled Fargo to gallop eastward along the gully. He knew it would not be long before the Utes guessed what he was up to, but by the time they fetched their horses he planned to be so far away that they had no hope of catching him.

Sixty feet the stallion traveled, to where a section of the gully had collapsed, forming an earthen ramp to the top. Fargo went up it without a pause and into the woods beyond. Leaning down, he shoved the Henry into the boot so both hands were free to work the reins. "Hang on tight!" he cried, and pushed the pinto to its limit one final time.

This was it. All or nothing. It would take the Utes five minutes or more to round up their scattered mounts. Fargo had to be long gone by then, or as far as the Ovaro could travel before exhaustion set in.

It helped that they were going downhill. Fargo's main

worry was that the stallion would step into a hole or a fissure. Going that fast made spotting hazards difficult. He constantly flicked his eyes from side to side.

A few errant shots were fired in their direction, but the shooters could not see them and were firing by sound alone. None of the bullets came anywhere close.

Soon they reached Treasure Creek. Fargo did not bother searching for a shallow spot to ford. He went right across. The water only came as high as the soles of his boots, sparing his sore left foot from being soaked. Once on the opposite bank, they plunged into the forest again.

Half an hour elapsed. Fargo had yet to see any trace of the war party. He stuck to the densest timber, never venturing across clearings or meadows where eagle eyes might detect them from afar.

At long last Fargo felt secure in reducing the stallion's gait to a walk. The pinto tossed its head a few times to show its displeasure at being ridden so hard for so long. Fargo hoped they would stumble on another waterway before too long, but thirty more minutes went by without sight of one.

An upland bench offered the big man a chance to scour the countryside and see how close the Utes were. In order to give the Ovaro a breather, he slid down and led the stallion up by the reins. He did not intend for Morning Flower to climb off, too, but she did. "There's no need for you—" he began.

"I can hold my own," the widow did not let him finish. "Your horse is very tired. The rest will do it good."

Fargo didn't press the point. "You did real well back there," he complimented her. "Better than most men I know could have done."

"Thank you for your compliment, but we would not have lived through it were it not for you." Morning Flower placed a hand on his arm. "You were magnificent. I have never seen anyone who can ride and shoot as you do. Not even my Joe." Her features grew pensive. "Well, maybe there is one man who can shoot like you do."

"Who?" Fargo asked absently as he trudged past an enormous boulder.

"Wolf Rollins."

Fargo's interest perked. "You've seen him handle those fancy pistols of his?"

"Once. In the Springs. Before all this trouble began. Joe took me there to buy supplies." Her eyes stared at the trees in their path but they were seeing the past. "Rollins and a few of his men were drinking and laughing. They set up bottles and shot at them to see who was the best. Wolf Rollins won easily." Blinking, she looked at Fargo. "He is quick with his hands, Skye, the quickest man I have ever seen. If you go up against him, I fear he would beat you."

"Thanks for having so much confidence in me," Fargo cracked.

Morning Flower dug her fingers into his arm. "I have never met a man more capable than you, not even my beloved Joe. But heed my words. Wolf Rollins is someone you should avoid if you can."

"I've never run from a fight, and I'm not about to start now."

The retort of a shot to the west brought their conversation to an end. Fargo cocked his head. Seconds later another shot echoed off the surrounding peaks, coming from further south.

"What does it mean?" Morning Flower questioned.

"My guess would be that they've split up to find us and are signaling back and forth," Fargo said. A third shot, well to the west, confirmed it.

The top of the bench was a two-acre rectangle, covered with pines for the most part. Not in the middle, though, where a hillock poked above the treetops. Fargo steered the Ovaro into the pines, then left the stallion there while he patrolled the rim, keeping well enough back that he could not be seen from below.

Few animals were abroad. The shots had driven almost all the game into hiding. To the north, grazing at the edge of a meadow, were five elk, one a massive bull with a gigantic rack. Above the snowcapped peak soared a hawk.

Of more interest to Fargo were the riders paralleling Treasure Creek. At that distance he could not distinguish much, other than the fact that there were a lot of them and they appeared to be hunting for something. He figured it had to be the Utes seeking tracks, although it could just as well be Wolf Rollins and the outlaws.

Morning Flower laughed. "Look at them! They will never overtake us now. We can relax."

Fargo didn't share her confidence. "Like hell," he said. "I'll relax when you're safe and sound with your cousins, not before."

"Do we go on, then?"

Five hours or more of daylight were left. Fargo was loath to waste a single minute, but he had the Ovaro to think of. Two days in a row the stallion had been ridden to the point of collapse. It could use all the rest it could get.

The deciding factor, though, was the group of dark clouds forming on the western horizon. Treasure Mountain was in for a late afternoon thunderstorm, a common occurrence in the Rockies. If heavy enough, the rain would obliterate their tracks. Tall Bear would have no choice but to give up.

"We'll rest here until morning," Fargo informed her, "provided we find some water. The pinto can't go the night without a drink."

Returning to the Ovaro, Fargo walked it toward the hillock, the one place on the bench where a spring might be located. The stallion seemed to verify his deduction by raising its head, pricking its ears toward the small hill, and snorting.

Morning Flower was thinking of something other than water. "Knowing Tall Bear as I do, it would not surprise me if he tears up everything I own before he goes back to the village," she mentioned. "It is bad enough I have lost my husband and my horse. Now this." She kicked at a dead branch in her way. "My Joe was fond of saying that life is never fair. I think now I understand why."

The pines thinned. A strip of grass ringed the hillock, dotted by huge boulders lying pell-mell, as if thrown about by a giant. The Ovaro sniffed loudly, nostrils flaring.

"I will go to the left," Morning Flower volunteered. "You go to the right. Whichever one of us discovers the spring first will give a yell."

Fargo did as she suggested. Many smaller boulders lay alone and in heaps, evidence of a geologic upheaval ages ago. Picking his way through them, he was rewarded by the sight of fresh deer tracks. The spring must be very close.

The Ovaro had the same idea. Increasing the length of its strides, it attempted to brush past Fargo, pushing at him with its muzzle. Fargo brought it up short with a tug on the reins. In its current state, the stallion was likely to drink until it was sick, if not watched closely. Even the best of horses had that tendency when overcome by dire thirst.

Then they rounded a boulder and in front of them glistened a sparkling clear pool. On the other side stood Morning Flower, acting amazed to see them.

"Why didn't you holler?" Fargo asked. Suddenly it dawned on him that she was looking beyond him, not at him. A feeling of dread coursed through him, even before he heard a mocking titter and a familiar voice.

"Why, hello again, sonny! Long time, no see. Did you miss me?"

11

Skye Fargo was growing sick and tired of having people hold him at gunpoint. Since he struck the San Juans, it had happened time and again. He was almost inclined to snap off a shot at Ike McDermott. Almost, but not quite. Because he knew that if he so much as twitched, the smirking midget would put a hole in him the size of an apple.

McDermott stood in a narrow space between two boulders, a gap so small that only he could have fit in it. His rifle was cocked and held as steady as could be. Chuckling, he emerged and wagged the Sharps at Morning Flower. "Come on around and join us, my dear," he said pleasantly. "We have a lot to talk about." To Fargo he said, "And would you be so kind as to shuck your hardware for me again, sonny? Same way you did before?"

"This is getting to be a habit," Fargo grumbled as he did.

McDermott shrugged. "It beats not breathing. Besides, I haven't really done you any harm, so you have no call to be so upset."

"Don't I?" Fargo countered. "If you think that you're dragging us back to your silver mine, think again. We won't go."

Morning Flower was leading her mare closer. "He speaks the truth, Ike. You betrayed my friendship. I do not know if I can ever trust you again."

The prospector was stung by her rebuke. Scrunching up his face, he said, "I was only trying to help you out, my dear. You know how fond I am of you. I would never deliberately do anything to jeopardize our friendship."

Fargo couldn't help it. He snorted and declared, "You damned idiot! You threatened to keep us prisoners in that cavern for the rest of our lives! Are we supposed to be *grateful?*"

To Fargo's surprise, McDermott let the Sharps droop. "Point taken," he said contritely. "I'll admit that it wasn't the smartest thing I've ever done. But taking her there was the only way I could think of to save her from Tall Bear." He paused, his facial muscles rippling as he waged an internal war. "As for the threats, chalk that up to stupidity. Once I actually got you there, I was so scared you'd try to steal my claim out from under me that I went a little bit loco."

The man appeared to be sincere, and some of Fargo's anger evaporated. "Why did you come after us, if not to haul us back?"

"That was my intent, at first," McDermott confessed. "But I had a lot of time to ponder while I was searching, and I saw that it wouldn't be right." He looked at the widow. This time the longing in his eyes was as plain as the nose on his face. "I would never want to hurt Morning Flower in any way. Believe me when I say I only want what is best for her."

Fargo had suspected as much, and now he knew. The prospector was in love with the Ute woman. "If you mean that, then you'll help me get her to safety. She wants to go live with her cousins, north of here a ways."

McDermott faced Morning Flower. "The ones who are living with Colorow's band?"

"Yes," she confirmed.

Fargo could tell the midget was not pleased by the prospect, since it meant McDermott would not get to see her very often, if at all. But the prospector put on a brave front.

"Well, that's for the best, I reckon. Colorow is a decent man. He doesn't look down his nose at all whites like Tall Bear does, so he won't hold it against you that you married Joe."

Morning Flower walked up to McDermott and tenderly put a hand on his shoulder. "You are welcome to come see me any time you want. Now that I understand why you did what you did, I can forgive you. My lodge will always be your lodge."

The man brightened, but not much. "I may just take you up on that." With an effort, he turned away from her, coughed a few times, and told Fargo, "You can pick up your guns. I just didn't want you to do anything rash before I had the chance to explain myself."

The whole time they had been talking, Fargo had been holding on to the Ovaro's reins. The stallion, impatient to get at the water, had repeatedly stamped its front hooves. Now Fargo let go, and the pinto promptly stepped to the spring, dipped its muzzle, and greedily drank in loud, noisy gulps.

"That reminds me," McDermott said. Sticking two fingers into his mouth, he whistled like a marmot. In seconds, Nightwind pranced through the boulders. McDermott stroked the pony and remarked, "I had just about given up on finding the two of you and was on my way back to my claim when I heard a lot of shooting a while ago." He nodded toward the west side of the bench. "Spotted you coming from a long way off."

"We tangled with Tall Bear," Fargo revealed. "Yesterday, it was Wolf Rollins and his boys. Both of them are on the lookout for us."

The prospector chuckled. "How does it feel to be so darned popular?"

It was then that a tremendously strong gust of wind shook the trees ringing the hill. A harbinger of the elemental fury to come, it reminded Fargo of the roiling black clouds that were rapidly approaching. He pulled his hat brim low to keep from losing it. "Know anywhere handy we can take shelter until the rain passes us by?" he asked.

"As a matter of fact, sonny, I do," McDermott said.

North of the spring was a wide deadfall caused by a previous storm. Pines had been toppled right and left, many falling over one another. At one point the downed trees formed a sort of gigantic lean-to large enough for the Ovaro to stand under.

The wind grew steadily stronger. It began to howl among the trunks and bend saplings as if they were twigs. Grass and weeds were whipped into a frenzy.

The dank smell of moisture was heavy in the air as Fargo

gathered enough dead wood to last the night. By the time he returned, Morning Flower and McDermott had fashioned a crude makeshift barrier of intertwined branches and brush that could be placed across the opening to shield them from the downpour.

The wind rose to a crescendo. Blue sky was devoured by black clouds until the blue was entirely gone. Light raindrops fell, pattering the earth gently at first but growing larger and larger as the minutes passed, until a steady downpour hammered the bench.

Some of the drops got through the deadfall above their heads, but not many. Fargo plugged a few open spots with branches and brush. Suddenly the wind died. The rain tapered to a drizzle. It was the lull before the storm, the few moments of quiet Nature granted those creatures still seeking sanctuary.

A crackling flash of lightning signaled the onslaught. The rain resumed with a vengance. The wind became a shrieking banshee. Thunder boomed without letup, rumbling back and forth across the sky. Raindrops as big as a man's thumbnail bombarded everything.

Fargo was glad. Peeking out through the barrier, he smiled as the rain churned barren patches of earth into so much mud. In no time at all, the trail he and Morning Flower had left would be erased without a trace. Tall Bear and Wolf Rollins could not possibly track them to the bench.

The widow sat by the small fire, arms looped around her knees, deep in thought. To one side, the prospector watched her silently, his sadness so heavy that it bowed his shoulders.

Fargo almost felt sorry for the man. It had to be hell, going through life half the size of those around you, more often than not the object of scorn and ridicule, never being treated as an equal.

A bolt of lightning seared the heavens close to their shelter and struck a tree with a blinding flash. Fargo saw the pine start to topple toward them, but at the last second a powerful blast of wind caused it to fall wide of the deadwood, smashing down with a huge thud.

It was warm and cozy there by the fire. Fargo looked at the widow, remembering the night before. The swell of her breasts as she leaned forward to poke at the fire was all it took to harden him like a rock, but he was not about to sidle up close to her with the prospector right there. McDermott might fly into a rage.

The thunderstorm lasted less than an hour. In its wake the land was left dripping wet, the air muggy. Fargo removed the barrier and stepped out to stretch and survey the bench. Birds were starting to sing again. A dusky four-legged form moved in the vicinity of the spring.

"Anyone want venison for supper?" Fargo asked, as he retrieved the Henry.

"We're staying here the night?" McDermott asked.

"That's the plan," Fargo said, and hurried off before the mule deer wandered elsewhere. He wasn't worried about the shot being heard by their enemies. The storm had not traveled all that far to the east. Distant thunder peeled constantly, and any gunfire would seem like part of it from a distance.

The deer was a ten-point buck, cautiously nearing the spring. Fargo saw it clearly as he came to the end of the pines. He fixed a bead, but the buck stepped past a boulder. From out of the high grass nearby a pair of does appeared. Fargo let them go. It was the buck he wanted.

Circling to the right, Fargo sought another glimpse of his quarry. He got it when the buck stepped between a pair of boulders, then halted to test the breeze. Fargo aimed, lightly pressed his finger to the trigger, and was about to fire when from somewhere behind him a horse nickered.

Fargo did not whirl or spring to the nearest cover or make any other abrupt movement that might draw attention. He simply sank slowly into a crouch and pivoted on his boot heels.

Four Utes had scaled the west side of the bench and were winding toward the hillock. Strung out in single file, they scoured the ground around them. Their frustration at not finding any tracks was conspicuous.

Quietly flattening, Fargo made like an eel and wriggled into a clump of brush. He reasoned that the four warriors must have been sent east of the creek by Tall Bear and found the Ovaro's prints before the thunderstorm hit. They had been able to tell that the stallion had been heading for the bench, and once the storm had passed them by, they had come to investigate.

Damn the luck! Fargo reflected, debating whether to try and drop them or to let them nose around a bit. If they found no sign, they might up and leave before too long.

Another consideration was the fact that where there were four Utes, others could be close by. Fargo had been wrong to assume that the entire war party was still west of Treasure Creek. It was a good thing he had not shot at the mule deer, as the shot might have brought Tall Bear and every last warrior on the run.

The Utes would pass by within forty feet of where Fargo lay. To reduce the risk of being spotted, he removed his hat and placed it close to his chest.

A stocky warrior packed with muscle was in the lead. He had a suspicious air about him and kept glancing at the underbrush as if he expected an ambush. Across his thighs rested a Spencer, a seven-shot rifle seeing more and more use by frontiersmen and Indians.

The third warrior was armed with a Volcanic Arms rifle, a model similar to Fargo's Henry but lacking the Henry's range and stopping power.

The other two had bows.

Fargo held himself rigid as they came even with the brush. One of them gazed in his direction but did not see him. He breathed a little easier when they had gone by. Then he glanced toward the deadfall.

Morning Flower had emerged from their shelter. Unaware of the Utes, she stood watching a pretty yellow and black butterfly flit about. She was in the shadow of several trees, so there was a good chance the Utes would not notice her if she stayed where she was.

Fargo saw the butterfly fly off toward the hill. Morning Flower took a few steps to keep it in sight. The strides brought her to the edge of the sunlight. She went to take one more, and her head jerked around. Thankfully, she had seen the Utes. But unlike Fargo, she dropped so fast that she rustled the grass around her.

The warrior with the Spencer instantly straightened and glanced to the north. He said something that caused the others to do the same.

Fargo tensed. No smoke showed above the deadfall, but the opening was visible as a murky dark patch. If he looked closely enough, he could just make out the white splotches on the Ovaro's coat, but that was only because he knew the stallion was there.

To the Utes, all would appear normal. Or so Fargo hoped. He could not see the fire from where he was, and he could only pray the pony and the pinto blocked the flames from the Utes' view. The four men had slowed and the lead rider was slanting toward the spot where Morning Flower had dropped down.

If it wasn't one thing, it was another, Fargo mentally noted as he aimed at the center of the foremost warrior's back. He marked the man's advance, and when the muscular Ute was almost to the point where Fargo was certain the man would see the widow, he prepared to fire.

At that juncture, from the area of the spring, there came a loud splash, as if the buck or one of the does had jumped into the pool to cool off.

It was all the Utes needed to hear. Reining their war horses, they galloped off. As soon as they were out of sight, Fargo rose and ran toward the deadfall, replacing his hat along the way. Morning Flower rose when he was only yards from her.

"I am sorry. I nearly gave us away."

"No harm done," Fargo said, scooping her hand into his and flying to the opening. The prospector was at the fire, filling a coffe pot. "No time for that," Fargo informed him, and explained.

Working together, they quickly smothered the flames. The coffee pot was stuffed into the prospector's saddlebags. Fargo moved to the opening with the Ovaro's reins in his left hand and his Colt in his right. There was no activity near the spring that he could see, so without delay he bore to the left, hurrying eastward to go around the deadwood.

Morning Flower hustled along close to the stallion's flank while McDermott brought up the rear.

Fargo did not take his eyes off the hill. He went over sixty feet and was nearing the forest when the buck and the two does burst from the boulders surrounding the spring and bounded off into the woods not ten yards from where he was. It was logical to conclude that the warriors had spooked them.

But it was more than that. The deer were still in sight when one of the Utes with a bow trotted into the open after them. The man had the same idea as Fargo had had earlier. But he forgot about the mule deer when he spied Fargo and the others.

Fargo raised the Colt as the warrior bellowed to his companions. The bow swung toward him, and a shaft was drawn back. Thumbing off a shot, Fargo was rewarded by the rider's jerking around and clutching a shoulder.

Slipping a boot into a stirrup, Fargo mounted. He held his arms down for Morning Flower to follow his example. McDermott's Sharps cracked. A piercing whinny erupted from the Ute's horse and it buckled, mortally stricken, spilling the warrior. Harsh yells from beyond the front ranks of boulders indicated that the others were on their way to help him.

Fargo did not let another second go by. Jabbing his spurs, he trotted into the pines. The pinto had not gotten the long rest it needed but it responded superbly, ready to gallop until it dropped if that was what he required.

A rifle banged. Looking back, Fargo saw the warrior with the Spencer working the trigger guard. The other two Utes had dismounted to help the wounded man.

Ike McDermott rode low over his custom-made, undersized saddle, an unnecessary precaution since his horse was so small that his head did not rise above the thickets surrounding them. It was unlikely the Utes could see him, let alone set their sights on him.

Fargo faced due north and rode as if their lives depended on it, and they did. The shots might attract the war party, and Fargo did not care to have to elude the entire band a second time. Luck had been a prime factor in his first escape, and no string of luck ran forever.

The pinto charged from cover onto an open belt of grass that bordered the north rim. Fargo drew rein and they slid to a stop close to the brink. Below, a steep precipice fell away to jagged rocks. "Is there another way down other than to the west?" he called out to the prospector.

McDermott nodded and assumed the lead, his swift pony flowing eastward. Fargo followed and soon learned that Nightwind was aptly named. The pony was as fleet as a hare, as crafty as a fox. It could get through narrow spaces no normal-sized horse dared attempt, and it could pass under trees so low that if Fargo tried to do the same he would be knocked for a loop by low limbs. He was hard-pressed to keep up.

It wasn't long before a switchback appeared, leading down into a valley. Miles to the east reared another less forested mountain. Fargo had the feeling that if they could only reach it, they would be safe.

All their troubles were centered on Treasure Mountain. That was where the prospector had struck it rich, where Wolf Rollins and his pack of killers were concentrating their search for the claim, and where the Utes were out in force seeking to kill any enemies they came across.

The switchback was rimmed with a growth of dense saplings, so many that Fargo found it hard going. He fell behind McDermott, whose smaller mount picked its way to the bottom before Fargo was halfway down. He expected the prospector to wait, but the midget rode off into a tract of woods fringing the valley floor.

"Where does he think he is going?" Morning Flower asked.

"Maybe he's changed his mind about helping to get you to Colorow's village," Fargo said. "Or maybe he just wants to scout the land ahead."

McDermott had yet to reappear when they came to the bottom. Fargo rose in the stirrups to survey the terrain. The woods were mostly pine, bordered by firs and aspens higher up. Lush grass, dappled by shadows of passing clouds, covered the rest of the valley. Sunset was about two hours off.

"I don't see him," Morning Flower said.

"He can't have gone far," Fargo said, trotting in the direction the prospetor had taken. With the Utes after them, he could not stop and wait for the man to return.

Moments after they were under cover, three of the four warriors drew rein on the rim of the bench. The wounded man was not with them. Fargo pulled behind a wide pine to observe what they would do next.

The muscular Ute with the Spencer did most of the talking and gesturing. Presently he started down, the warrior armed with the Vulcan Arms rifle tagging along. The third man went back, most likely to stay with their wounded fellow.

Even though the odds were much more in his favor, Fargo preferred to avoid another clash if it were at all possible. He rode on, following the sign made by Nightwind. The prospector had headed due east at a brisk clip, as if he had a certain destination in mind.

Minutes passed without incident. Fargo, closely watching the forest before them, saw a pair of ravens abruptly take wing about five hundred yards distant. The big black birds flapped in ever-widening circles, squawking irately. They had been startled by something. Maybe McDermott.

"Skye!" Morning Flower urgently whispered.

The two Utes to their rear, pushing their animals at a feverish pace, were gaining rapidly. Fargo glimpsed them only briefly, but that was more than enough. Bringing the Ovaro to a gallop, he went over a low rise and found himself in a dry, rocky wash. He began to climb the other side. Inspiration struck, and when he reached the top he turned to the left, hastening into a thicket.

Fargo stopped and ducked. The pair of warriors pounded up to the wash and went down into it without a moment's hesitation. They goaded their mounts up the other side just as recklessly, gained the lip, and raced on into the forest without verifying that it was where the Ovaro's tracks led.

Morning Flower giggled softly. "You've lost them!"

Fargo was not so sure. It wouldn't take the Utes long to

realize they had made a mistake and turn around. Tugging on the reins, he rode northward, holding the stallion to a brisk pace, but not a gallop. It wasn't wise to wear the stallion out.

Suddenly, to the east, war whoops erupted. A rifle boomed and was answered by others. There was a lot of yipping and screeching, as Indians liked to do when chasing someone down. More shots rang out.

"I have a bad feeling," Morning Flower said, gripping his arm tightly.

A hill barred their way. Fargo swung around to the far side, then made for the top. Yards below the crest, the two of them slid from the saddle. On elbows and knees they climbed the rest of the way.

The widow gazed out over the valley first and sucked in a breath. "Oh, why didn't he stay with us?" she whispered.

Fargo had a fair idea of what he would see before he looked.

Ike McDermott had blundered into the rest of the Ute war party. He had fled as far as the valley floor, where a shot had brought down Nightwind. Now McDermott was bent over his cherished pony, blubbering like a baby, while the laughing Utes closed in. He turned on them but they pounced before he could unlimber his pistol. By sheer force of numbers the warriors overwhelmed him.

It was interesting to Fargo that they took the prospector alive. There could only be one reason. A grisly, gory one, with a bloody ending.

Morning Flower gripped his wrist. "Tall Bear will torture him! Despite all Ike has done, we can not let that happen!"

"What do you suggest we do?" Fargo felt obligated to ask, even though he knew he would not like her answer.

"What else?" the Ute woman rejoined. "We must stick close to them, and when we see our chance, free him."

Fargo said nothing. He didn't have to. She wasn't stupid. Morning Flower knew that her plan could very well get them both killed.

12

Over the Continental Divide, in a remote nook of the Rockies no white man had ever set eyes on before, lay a small, pristine lake. The Utes took the prospector there. Fargo did not know why. He asked Morning Flower but she was equally puzzled. His best guess was that Tall Bear wanted an out-of-the-way place to conduct the torture.

They shadowed the war party up and over Wolf Creek Pass, then on through heavy timber to a high country basin. Even at night, the lake at its center stood out, its surface shimmering darkly like a mirror, reflecting the twinkling stars and the moon.

It was past midnight when the Utes got there. They promptly constructed conical lodges made from long, slender tree limbs, and settled in for the night.

From a shelf overlooking the lake shore, Fargo caught glimpses of Ike McDermott. All the fight had gone out of the man. When the Utes manhandled him, he did not complain. When a few abused him with hard blows, he did not resist. The prospector sat slumped over, his posture that of someone who no longer gave a damn whether he lived or died.

McDermott was not taken into any of the lodges. A heavy pole was pounded into the earth and he was tied to it, bound at the chest and the ankles.

Two warriors were left to stand guard when the rest turned in. The pair made a small fire and huddled close to it. Every now and again one or the other would get up to check the string of tethered mounts.

Dancing firelight played over Ike McDermott. He sagged

against the coils of rope like one already dead, his blank gaze fixed on the bare patch of earth at his feet.

"What is the matter with him?" Fargo whispered. "Where there's life, there's hope. He shouldn't give up so soon."

"The loss of his pony has broken his spirit," Morning Flower said. "Did you not notice? He loved Nightwind more than any person has ever loved any horse. Many times I heard him say that the pony was his best friend in all the world, as he put it. He even let Nightwind sleep next to him at night."

Fargo had known the prospector was attached to the animal, he just hadn't realized how deep the attachment ran. "If we're going to get him out of there, we have to do it now."

"But the two warriors—" Morning Flower began.

"Are the only two awake," Fargo pointed out, and told her what he had in mind. She listened attentively, frowning when he was done.

"We must not make any mistakes or we will end up in their clutches, as well."

Fargo didn't need to be reminded. Patting her leg, he glided to the right. On his stomach, he slipped from the shelf down into scrub brush. Here there were twigs to avoid, and Fargo had to take care not to rustle the stems.

The two Utes were talking in low tones, one munching on what appeared to be pemmican.

Cottonwoods flourished close to the lake. It was toward them that Fargo carefully made his way. Once he froze when one of the warriors turned to rake the slope with a probing stare, as if the man suspected something was amiss. But in a few seconds the Ute resumed talking to his friend.

Fargo was close to the trees when the same warrior stood to make a circuit of the camp. Cradling a rifle, he strolled past the horses to the lake, satisfied his thirst, and came around behind the temporary lodges to a spot directly across from the cottonwoods.

Screened by high grass and the trees, Fargo had no fear of being discovered but then the warrior came straight toward him, prompting Fargo to wonder if maybe the Ute sensed his presence. His right hand closed on the butt of his Colt, but he waited to see what the warrior would do.

The man stopped near the trees and bent a knee. He poked and pried at some stones littering the shore. Holding one that seemed to be quartz, he crossed to his companion.

Fargo crawled into the cottonwoods. He was now at the border of the vegetation, less than fifteen feet from the lake and about the same distance from the nearest lodge off to his left. The fire was twice as far away.

Ike McDermott had not moved since being tied. His hat was gone, his hair tousled. His shirt had been torn and there was a long rip on his left pant leg.

Fargo thought of trying to get McDermott's attention but decided against it. In the prospector's befuddled state, there was no telling what McDermott might do. Maybe he would call out, alerting the Utes.

Minutes dragged by. Fargo had advised the widow to give him enough time to get into position before she played out her part in their bid to rescue the midget.

The warriors were swapping tales, chuckling and joking. Neither appeared the least bit sleepy. Both leaped to their feet when a soft whisper hailed them from the darkness. Spinning, they raised their weapons but did not use them. The tallest responded.

Morning Flower was no more than a vague shadow perched on the slope leading up to the bench. She spoke again, her silken voice held so low that it was unlikely she would awaken any of the sleepers in the lodges.

The two guards moved to the edge of the rocky shore. One spoke crisply and beckoned for the widow to come down. Morning Flower obeyed, but only halfway. Halting, she addressed them at length. Whatever she said appeared to allay their fears because they lowered their weapons and moved to meet her.

It was the moment Fargo had been waiting for. Slipping from the cottonwoods, he sped parallel to the vegetation until he was to the rear of the two warriors, in the very spot they had been standing moments before. He had made no noise. They were unaware anyone else was there. Just as he had planned.

Morning Flower went on talking, not stopping to take a breath, a rush of words meant to distract the husky warriors and prevent them from hearing Fargo's stealthy approach as he tiptoed toward them from the rear. When they stopped, so did he.

The tall Ute was growing angry. He gestured more sharply than before.

The widow did not lose her composure. She motioned at the lodges and said something that made the shorter warrior snicker. The tall one took a few more steps, bringing him face to face with Morning Flower. He was not amused. Grabbing her by the arm, he shifted to push her ahead of him.

Fargo drew the Colt. A few more steps were all he needed to get within striking range, and he brought the barrel crashing down on the short Ute's skull with all the force he could muster. The man crumpled, but not soundlessly. An agonized groan escaped his lips.

The tall Ute heard. He let go of Morning Flower and whirled, his rifle rising.

Fargo attacked. He wanted to club the man senseless but he wasn't close enough. The only way he could drop the warrior was to shoot. It would wake up the rest of the war party, forcing Morning Flower and him to flee, or suffer the same fate as McDermott.

The quick-thinking widow was not to be denied. Lunging, she shoved the tall Ute with one hand, as she wrenched the rifle from his grasp with the other. The warrior stumbled forward, dropping to one knee almost at Fargo's feet. Fargo swung a terrific blow that should have dropped the man like a poled ox, but the Ute twisted his head at the last instant and the barrel glanced off his brow, sending him staggering but not knocking him out. Fargo swept his arm back for another blow.

The tall Ute suddenly hurled himself at Fargo's legs. They both fell, Fargo on the bottom, the Ute's fingers seeking and finding his throat. Steely fingertips gouged into his neck, into his windpipe. Fargo slammed the Colt against the man's temple but it was like striking granite. The warrior vigorously shook his head to clear it.

Morning Flower leaped to Fargo's aid. She clubbed the tall Ute over the back of the head hard enough to stagger a bull buffalo, but all he did was sag briefly, then go on strangling Fargo.

Sucking in a ragged breath, Fargo smashed the warrior twice, the second time splitting skin and drawing blood. The warrior was stunned and weakening rapidly, but not fast enough to suit Fargo. He drove a knee into the man's midsection, and when the Ute doubled in half, rained four more resounding blows upon him.

Grunting, the tall Ute sprawled unconscious, pinning Fargo's legs. Fargo kicked the man off and rose, his pulse pounding. That had been much too close. It was no wonder, he mused, that the Utes had a reputation for being fierce fighters.

"Are you all right?" Morning Flower whispered.

"Fine," Fargo answered, although the truth was that his throat felt as if it had just been stomped by an enraged moose. He hurried to the shore, the widow dogging his steps.

No sound came from within any of the lodges.

Ike McDermott did not react when Morning Flower hustled to the stake and produced her knife. He made no comment as she furiously sawed at the loops around his chest, nor did he say a word when the rope fell off.

Fargo, covering her, saw several of the war horses swing their heads around. If any of the animals let out a loud whinny, it was bound to bring a few Utes into the open to investigate. The wind, thank goodness, was blowing his scent away from the string.

The widow bent lower, in order to cut the rope binding the prospector's ankles.

McDermott showed some sign of life, his head jerking as if he had been stung. Blinking, he stared at her and blurted out, "Morning Flower?"

"Hush!" the Ute woman cautioned. "The warriors will hear you and we will all be caught."

"The bastards!" McDermott said vehemently. "They shot poor Nightwind out from under me!"

"I know!" Morning Flower said while frantically slicing. "But listen to me! You must keep your voice down! We are all in great danger!"

McDermott did not seem to care. Fargo saw him glance at the lodges and open his mouth to shout. Whirling, Fargo slugged the prospector on the jaw, a solid punch that rocked McDermott and left him slumped against the pole.

Morning Flower had recoiled in shock. "Was that necessary?" she whispered.

Fargo did not bother to answer. They had to get out of there before any of the Utes woke up. Scanning the lodges, he knelt in front of McDermott. Morning Flower finished slicing. With a tug, he draped the limp prospector over his left shoulder just as a head appeared in the opening of a lodge on the right.

A sleepy warrior yawned, a yawn that froze on his face when he saw the three of them. He threw back his head to shout.

Fargo shot him. Rising, he backpedaled, swinging his Colt from shelter to shelter, ready to fire at the first thing that moved. Another head poked out of a different lodge, along with a rifle barrel. Without breaking stride, Fargo cored the man's brain.

Morning Flower stayed at his side, ready to help in any way she could. She had left her rifle on the shelf, so she could not back him up.

A third Ute materialized. A shot boomed. The slug zinged between the two of them. As the shooter started to emerge, Fargo hammered a single shot to the chest, flipping the man back inside.

Shouts broke out in every lodge. Someone bellowed commands that could barely be heard above the uproar.

The moment Fargo came to the brush, he whirled and pumped his legs up the slope. Lead smacked into the dirt on both sides, clipping leaves and limbs from the bushes. He gave Morning Flower a shove, saying, "You go first!"

War whoops and squeals of outrage replaced the bedlam

as more and more of the Utes realized their captive was being whisked away right under their noses.

Fargo looked back. Seven or eight Utes were outside, some examining those already shot, some making for the slope, still others heading for the horse string. Pivoting, he fanned the Colt twice. With each shot, a warrior dropped. The rest scattered for cover.

Dashing higher, Fargo plowed through weeds. Something snagged his boot and he nearly fell. As he regained his balance, shots peppered the slope.

Morning Flower was almost to the shelf. She motioned for him to hurry.

Fargo was doing his best. He had emptied the Colt and could not slow to reload. To make a bad situation even worse, McDermott picked that moment to revive.

The prospector groaned and then moved, feebly at first but with mounting urgency. Kicking and thrashing, he thundered, "What the hell! Who is carrying me?"

The shelf was mere yards above them. Fargo scrambled the rest of the distance, gaining the top as McDermott began to pummel his head and shoulders.

"Let go of me, damn you! I can stand on my own two feet!"

Fargo dumped him. The prospector squawked and tumbled as Fargo spun to confront the Utes. A full half-dozen were in determined pursuit. He was about to sink down and reload his pistol when his Henry was shoved in front of his face.

"I thought you might need this," Morning Flower said, grinning. She also had her own rifle.

There was already a cartridge in the chamber. Fargo tucked the stock to his shoulder and sent a slug into the nearest warrior. Then, with uncanny speed and precision, he unleashed a volley that withered the charging Utes like stalks of grain before a scythe. Beside him the widow fired once, toppling a warrior with an upraised lance.

The remaining Utes immediately hugged the ground, a few snapping off shots but none willing to expose themselves to Fargo's unerring marksmanship.

Two men on horseback were exceptions. Shrieking and

firing arrows just as fast as they could notch shafts, they galloped like madmen toward the shelf.

"Get down!" Fargo directed, grabbing Morning Flower by the wrist and yanking to make sure she did. Arrows whizzed above them. She started to reload but he stopped her by pressing his mouth to her ear and telling her what she must do next. Nodding, she scooted toward the rear of the shelf, pulling McDermott along with her.

Fargo dropped onto his side at the rim. The two Utes were still coming. They rushed past a warrior who tried to stop them from making the mistake they were about to make. Fargo imitated a log, the drumming of hooves growing louder, the rumble of the ground like that caused by a far off earthquake. The pair flew onto the shelf on either side of him. One noticed him, the other had eyes only for Morning Flower and McDermott.

Rolling, Fargo fired as the Ute who had seen him twisted to let loose a shaft. The slug caught the man below the jaw and heaved him clear off his horse. The other warrior, about to put an arrow into the widow, stiffened and whipped around. Fargo only had to elevate the barrel a fraction and squeeze the trigger.

Both Utes were down. Their horses turned to run off. Fargo sprang for the nearest, hollering to the widow, "Catch the other one!" He nabbed the rope reins on the fly and dug in his heels to prevent the animal from fleeing.

Morning Flower did not fare as well. She snatched hold of the other mount's mane and was almost wrenched off her feet when the horse wheeled. She had to let go.

Ike McDermott galvanized into action and gave chase. He was no match for the fleet war horse which sailed down the slope as if its hooves were endowed with wings.

Fargo was disappointed but there was nothing else he could do. "Get on!" he instructed the widow, and she lost no time swinging up.

The prospector had turned. "You too!" Fargo declared. Swiftly, he gave McDermott a boost. Once they were both safely on, he bounded to the Ovaro and forked leather.

Two thirds of the war party were surging up through the brush, firing as they advanced.

"Ride!" Fargo ordered, giving their horse a hard smack on the rump. It lit out of there as if its tail were ablaze and he followed, squeezing off shots to deter the onrushing Utes.

The forest was a murky maze of trunks and limbs and boulders that no sane person would risk at night. The moon helped, but not enough to illuminate every hazard. Morning Flower slowed, afraid of a fatal misstep, so Fargo shot past her. "Stay close!" he said. "We can shake them if we ride hard and fast."

"I will be right behind you!" the widow pledged.

Fargo rode like the proverbial wind, the feral howls of the Utes spurring him on. They were incensed and would not stop, short of dying or completely losing the trail.

On reaching the crest of the basin, Fargo slowed long enough to shove the Henry into the saddle scabbard. Morning Flower was proving as good as her word.

A large body of Utes raised pale puffs of dust a few hundred feet off. The warriors had stopped whooping and shrieking and buckled down to their deathly grim chore of catching up.

Fargo headed westward, toward Wolf Creek Pass. The Continental Divide reared above them, a stark series of majestic peaks, immense landmarks he could rely on to guide him right to the pass. He had no plan other than getting the widow and the prospector to safety. That in itself would tax his skill to its limit.

The clatter of hooves echoed off adjacent mountains, mingling with occasional guttural coughs of roaming grizzly bears and the piercing screams of roving mountain lions.

The steep climb wearied the horses rapidly. Fargo dropped to a trot after a couple of miles, and later on to a walk. By then the war party had fallen far back but was still in sight. Tall Bear, he figured, was being canny by conserving the war horses for later on.

Fargo had gone so long without decent sleep that he found himself nodding off if he did not make a conscious effort to the contrary. He would have given anything for six hours of undisturbed slumber. Morning Flower had to share his fatigue, yet she did not show it. She had an inner reservoir of energy that was remarkable.

Fargo did not keep track of the passing of time. He idly noted the changing positions of the stars and constellations. Only when the location of the North Star revealed that it had to be past three in the morning did he appreciate how long they had been riding. And how far they had yet to go until they reached Wolf Creek Pass.

On top of a ridge covered with firs, Fargo drew rein. Kneeing the Ovaro into the shadows, he secured the reins to a limb. As he filled his hands with the Henry once more, he heard Morning Flower and McDermott ride up.

"What are you doing?" She sounded upset.

Fargo did not turn. "Keep on going. I'll overtake you before noon if all goes well."

"You can not fight them by yourself."

"We have to end it before the sun comes up or we'll never shake them." Avoiding her gaze, Fargo skirted the war horse. She stuck out a smooth leg to stop him.

"It is not right that you do this alone. It is because of us that they seek your life. We will stay and help."

Fargo shook his head. "Ike doesn't have a rifle. He wouldn't be of much use."

Morning Flower could be as stubborn as any woman alive when she wanted to be. "Lend him your pistol. We will make sure they do not sneak around behind you."

McDermott, who had been strangely quiet, broke in. "Maybe he has the right notion, my dear. Your safety must come before all else."

The woman turned on him. "How can you think of leaving Skye alone to face them after what he has done for you? I could not have saved you alone."

"Believe me," the prospector said earnestly, "I am more grateful than words can say. But by the same token, saving my hide won't amount to a hill of beans if you're killed on my account. You mean more to me than my own life ever could."

Morning Flower pressed against the saddle horn to dismount. "We are not leaving!" she insisted.

Locking her foot into the stirrup, Fargo thwarted her.

"Your friend is right. If Tall Bear were to get his hands on you, everything we've done will have been for nothing." Cracking a grin, he waved at the peaks. "So don't be so ornery, woman. Light a shuck."

The lovely Ute burst into quiet tears. Fargo refused to give in and stepped aside so they could go on.

Ike leaned around her to grasp the reins. A tear splashed onto his cheek and he glanced up in bewilderment. Then he studied Fargo as if seeing him for the very first time. "Well, now. Isn't this interesting. The story of my life. I'm always the last to know."

"Get her out of here."

The prospector did. Morning Flower tried to stop him but McDermott's size was no measure of his strength. He would not relinquish the reins and in moments they were lost in the night.

Fargo moved to the brink of the east slope to make his stand. The war party climbed in small groups. In the lead cluster, his lean figure head and shoulders above the rest, was Tall Bear. Hunkering, Fargo reloaded, taking his time. The last cartridge went into the tubular magazine as the Utes paused just below his hiding place.

Tall Bear rose to scan the crest—and saw him.

13

Skye Fargo did not stop to think of the hopeless odds against him. He did not stop to dwell on the fact that it would be a miracle if he got out of there alive. The instant Tall Bear saw him, he took quick aim at the warrior's chest, thumbed back the hammer of his Henry, and stroked the trigger.

Yet as fast as Fargo fired, Tall Bear proved to be faster. The wily Ute let go of the reins and threw himself from his mount a fraction of a second before the rifle boomed. He was hit, but low down on the side instead of in the heart as Fargo had intended.

Upon hearing the blast, the war party exploded into a flurry of activity. Those with rifles began firing at the crest. Even though they had no clear target to shoot at, gunsmoke from the Henry gave them a fair idea of where Fargo was. Most worked their rifles while scattering to seek cover, so few of their shots were accurate.

A handful galloped toward the rim, converging on the spot where they believed Fargo to be, banging away as they charged.

Fargo dropped onto his stomach. So much lead hummed and buzzed above him that if he had not fallen flat, he would have been turned into a human sieve. He sighted on the bunch sweeping toward him. His first round punched the lead warrior into space. A second shot catapulted another Ute backward. The others promptly swerved to the right and the left.

Rolling to one side, Fargo aimed again, this time at a knot of men streaking wide to the south in order to flank him. He brought down the foremost rider, who fell in front of the rest. They frantically tried to avoid trampling him, and in doing so two of them collided and their mounts crashed to the earth in a tangle of limbs and warriors. Those still on horseback sped toward nearby trees.

In the swirl of violence, Fargo had lost sight of Tall Bear. And it was the Ute leader Fargo wanted to bring down most of all. Tall Bear was the one who would not leave Morning Flower alone. If he were eliminated, the rest might decide that she was not worth the loss of so many lives and go on back to their village.

As abruptly as it had begun, the firing stopped. The Utes had all vanished as if swallowed by the earth, but Fargo knew better. They had blended into the trees and boulders and clumps of weeds as skillfully as Apaches. Now they were trying to pinpoint him. When that failed, they would try to reach the crest without being spotted. Some, no doubt, would again attempt to outflank him and come up on him from the rear.

Despite knowing all this, Fargo stayed where he was. He was going to buy Morning Flower and the prospector as much time as he could.

An inky silhouette appeared briefly a score of yards lower, then disappeared. Another dark shape snaked from one cluster of brush to a different one. Yet a third figure stepped boldly into view from behind a tree and stood there for a full five seconds before ducking behind the trunk again.

Fargo grinned. The Utes were crafty devils. They were deliberately showing themselves. They wanted him to open fire again so they could determine his exact position.

Another warrior brazenly exposed himself and took his sweet time ducking down.

Elsewhere there were hints of furtive movement. Other warriors were snaking closer without exposing themselves.

Acting on impulse, Fargo pulled back from the rim, rose but stayed low, and padded northward two dozen yards. From his new vantage point he could see many of the Utes slinking toward the middle of the ridge. One of them was quite close to the spot he had vacated. Aligning the Henry, he fired.

Fireflies sparkled all along the slope as rifles and a few carbines cracked in reply. Utes who realized they could be seen, hid.

Fargo limited himself to four shots. Then, crawling back to relative safety, he rose again and ran to the south. His strategy was to never stay in any one place too long, in order to keep the Utes guessing. It would keep them from picking him off. He hoped.

Someone began barking commands. It sounded like Tall Bear. Fargo veered toward the rim, anxious to locate the cause of all the bloodshed and give the Ute his due. The shouts stopped as he snuck forward to survey the mountainside.

There was no movement below. It was as if all the Utes had frozen in place. Fargo inched farther out to scour the grass and weeds that grew along the crest, but saw no trace of any warriors. Puzzled, he moved to the rear and rose up on his right knee.

The Utes would not just give up. They had to be up to something, Fargo knew, but what? Were they going to wait for daylight? Or did they have something else in mind?

A low nicker from the Ovaro gave Fargo his answer. The Utes were waiting, all right, but they were waiting for something to happen in the next few seconds. He had already been outflanked! Someone was behind him!

Fargo dived to the left, twisting as he sprang. A rifle cracked, the slug kicking dirt where his boots had been. A burly Ute in a breechcloth and nothing else stood twenty feet away. The man swiveled to take aim for another shot.

The Henry was tucked against Fargo's side. He fired from the hip, a snap shot intended for the Ute's chest. Instead, as much to his amazement as the Ute's, the slug struck the warrior's rifle, splintering the stock and knocking the weapon from the man's hands. The startled Ute grabbed for a long knife at his hip.

In a twinkling Fargo was on his feet, the Henry pointed at the warrior's head. The man stiffened, his hand on the bone hilt. Wagging the Henry, Fargo indicated that the Ute should raise both arms. Reluctantly, the warrior did.

Fargo moved closer. Another idea had occurred to him,

and he asked, without any real hope of getting an answer, "I don't suppose you speak the white man's tongue?"

"Yes. Little bit, white dog."

Elated, Fargo shifted sideways so he could keep an eye on the crest. It would not be long before the Utes realized he was still alive and came at him with everything they had. "Why are your warriors throwing their lives away for no reason?" he asked.

The Ute's dark eyes narrowed. "What you mean?"

"I do not want to fight your people. I came to Ute country in peace. I only wanted to pass through. It is Tall Bear who started the trouble. All because I made friends with Morning Flower." Fargo paused. "You know how he feels about her."

"We all know," the warrior said, and he did not sound very happy about it.

Fargo, encouraged, talked quickly, never knowing when they might be interrupted by a blaze of gunfire. "Tall Bear is to blame for all this. He is the one who wants her. Morning Flower has told him many times that she does not want to live in his lodge, yet he will not take no for an answer."

The Ute's furrowed brow showed that he was mulling over the points being made.

"I know a little of Ute customs," Fargo went on. "Like the Apaches, I know that one Ute warrior can challenge another to formal combat in order to right a wrong. Is this not true?"

"Yes," the Ute said suspiciously.

"I have heard that once the Utes and the Navajos settled a dispute by having a warrior from each tribe fight to the death. Is this true, too?"

"Yes. Maybe do again. Navajos say hot springs belong them. But belong my people."

Fargo got right to the point. "Then go back and tell the others that I challenge Tall Bear to formal combat."

The warrior stared.

"I know I am not a Ute, but that should not make a difference. I am the one who has been wronged. I never wanted this fight. Tall Bear forced it on me. If he wants me dead, then he should try to kill me himself and not let other warriors die on his account."

For tense moments the warrior did not so much as twitch. Fargo was afraid his request had fallen on deaf ears, that because he was white, the Ute would not take it seriously.

"I say your words, white man. Maybe Tall Bear fight. Maybe not." The warrior boldly walked toward the rim, pausing to glance at Fargo. The corners of his mouth curled. "You sly, like fox."

Fargo trailed him to the crest. The Ute called out in his own tongue and was answered by warriors below. Not showing any fear of being shot in the back, the warrior bounded down the slope and into a stand of trees, shouting as he ran. Others rose from concealment to go join him. Many looked up at Fargo but none opened fire.

Now all Fargo could do was wait. The council might take minutes. Or it might take hours. Whichever way, he wouldn't budge until they gave him an answer.

Fargo was no fool. He knew full well the risk he was taking. Even if Tall Bear agreed, he had to defeat the tall warrior in ritual combat, which meant a fight to the death using knives. Some cowboy friends of his would brand his play a fool's proposition. But Fargo judged differently. He owed Morning Flower a debt, and he intended to repay it the best way he knew how, by ridding her of the bastard who wanted to force himself on her.

Loud voices broke out. The Utes were arguing. Loudest among them was the raspy voice of Tall Bear.

Fargo crouched, the Henry across his thighs, and leisurely replaced the spent cartridges. One of the horses that had gone down was still down, making horrible choking sounds. The animal needed to be put out of its misery but Fargo was not about to do the job when the Utes might misconstrue the shot. He bided his time.

A check of the slopes above revealed no sign of the widow and the prospector. Fargo flattered himself that they were long gone, safely on their way northward to the village where Morning Flower's cousins lived.

By Fargo's reckoning it was about forty minutes after his

palaver with the burly warrior that the Utes emerged from the trees in a compact group. At its head was the man he had talked to, and Tall Bear. The tall warrior walked stiffly and had his left hand pressed to his side.

Fargo straightened as the war party came to a stop. He was careful to dip the barrel of his rifle to the ground, but he kept his thumb on the hammer and a finger resting on the trigger. "Is my challenge accepted?" he asked.

The burly warrior answered. "It is, white man. But—" He stopped, evidently trying to find the right words. "Tall Bear be hurt. It not fair him fight you when you not."

Fargo locked eyes with the man who had caused him so much trouble. "What does Tall Bear want to do?"

"Him say—" the burly Ute said, and again had to stop. "Him say you tie one arm. Then he fight you." The man bent his own behind him to demonstrate. "This way."

Fargo saw a smug look come over Tall Bear. The warrior was counting on him to decline, and once he backed down, Tall Bear would tell the others that he had never really wanted a fair fight, that it was all a trick. Tall Bear would have no problem inciting the war party into resuming hostilities. But Fargo had a surprise for him. "Let Tall Bear know that I agree to his terms."

The spokesman appeared confused.

"Yes," Fargo clarified. "We will do it the way he wants."

Some of Tall Bear's smugness vanished when the answer was translated. He nodded curtly, then angled to the left to climb to the top, his hand still over the wound.

Fargo backed up, turned, and walked to the Ovaro. The Henry went into the boot. Drawing the Colt, he shoved it into a saddlebag. Footsteps let him know someone was approaching.

The Ute who knew English held a coiled grass rope. "I tie arm, white man."

"There's no need for that," Fargo nodded at the rope. To show why, he turned and slipped his left forearm under the middle of his belt. "See? I will keep it there the whole time."

"You not cheat, white man," the Ute warned, gesturing at

the other warriors, who had formed a long line along the rim. "They not like."

"Do they agree to the terms?" Fargo said.

"Terms? What that word?"

"If I win, the rest of you mount up and go back to your village. Morning Flower is to be left in peace. And no one from your band is to bother her ever again."

The Ute frowned. "You not say this before."

With good reason, Fargo reflected. He had not wanted Tall Bear to have an excuse to decline the challenge. Now that the tall warrior was committed, it would shame him if he backed out. "Go let them know."

"What if Tall Bear win?" the Ute inquired.

Fargo chuckled. "Then I guess you and your friends get to carve me into little pieces or take my hair or whatever else suits you."

"Forget one thing. We also take horse and guns and all you have," the Ute noted, giving the stallion an appreciative once-over.

"That fair enough for you?" Fargo asked.

"For me," the Ute responded. "Cannot say how rest think." Hefting the rope, he departed.

Fargo saw that Tall Bear had drawn a big knife and was limbering up by taking practice swings. The knife wasn't a bowie but it was almost as large, while the blade was the very best tempered steel, not the inferior metal often used in trade knives.

The warriors gathered around the burly Ute. It did not take long for them to come to an understanding, although once again Tall Bear argued loudly. The spokesman came back. "They say fight go on. They say if you win, they not bother Morning Flower."

"Then let's get it over with," Fargo declared. Since Tall Bear stood to the north, he stepped to the south and halted about ten paces away. Stooping, he palmed the Arkansas toothpick.

The burly Ute laughed. "You fight Tall Bear with that small thing? Maybe you want die, eh?" He moved off to mingle with his fellows and must have repeated his remark in their own language because they roared with rowdy mirth.

Fargo let Tall Bear make the first move. When the warrior started toward him, he advanced, balancing his weight on the balls of his feet. He held the toothpick below his waist, close to his leg.

Tall Bear moved in slowly, grinning. He had good cause. His knife was much bigger and his arms a lot longer, giving him a much greater reach. In a knife fight, that counted for half the battle.

Fargo turned so that his left side was presented to his enemy. Now Tall Bear could barely see the toothpick, and it rattled him. The warrior repeatedly glanced down at Fargo's leg, just as Fargo had intended.

The war party had fallen completely silent. With eager, hawkish faces they tensed for the clash.

Bending his knees a little more, Fargo halted. His shorter reach lent itself more to defense than attack, and he had to be ready for the first thrust. It came with the blinding speed of a striking sidewinder. Tall Bear put all he had into a lancing strike aimed at Fargo's throat, but he telegraphed the blow by shifting his shoulders before he struck. Fargo, twisting, parried with the toothpick, then skipped aside as Tall Bear tried to decapitate him.

For a man who pretended to be gravely wounded, Tall Bear was remarkably quick and agile. As he circled to find an opening, it became clear why. His left hand fell to his side, revealing that the bullet had dug a shallow furrow in his flesh, nothing more. His vitals had been spared. He was in no danger of dying. Far from it. And having duped Fargo into using only one arm, he was free to use both of his as he saw fit.

Fargo would have been justified in sliding his left hand from under his belt. But it would break his word to the Utes. It also might earn him an arrow in the back from any friend of Tall Bear's so inclined. So he fought with only his right arm, parrying a series of stabs, both high and low.

Fargo could see what the warrior was doing. Tall Bear was taking his measure, gauging his skill, testing him to see if he had any weaknessess. He retreated to make the Ute think that he was being hard pressed but Tall Bear did not take the bait and closed in.

The row of warriors had yet to utter a peep. They were riveted to the combat, as white men would be to a pistol duel. A few fingered weapons but made no attempt to use them.

All of this Fargo took in while dancing out of the way of an overhand swing meant to cleave his head like a melon. Their blades rang together. Pivoting, Fargo slashed at Tall Bear's right wrist, and connected.

The warrior snarled and leaped out of reach. He stared at the blood dripping from the cut as if he could not believe his eyes. Then, switching the big knife to his left hand, he stalked forward, intent on a kill.

Fargo waved the Arkansas toothpick in a small circle, feinted, and speared the point at Tall Bear's abdomen. Tall Bear lowered the big blade to counter. At that very moment, Fargo drove the toothpick lower yet, at the warrior's thigh, but Tall Bear wrenched to the right, suffering only a deep gash.

Some of the Utes were whispering among themselves. One man extended a carbine toward Fargo and had it swatted away by another warrior.

The new wound provoked Tall Bear into a frenzy. With wild swings he drove Fargo backward, chopping again and again at Fargo's head and neck. The big blade battered the slim toothpick, nearly tearing the knife from Fargo's grasp. To gain breathing space, Fargo ducked and stabbed at Tall Bear's groin. The tall Ute reacted as if he were a jackrabbit.

Fargo stayed low to the ground and circled. Having lost track of where they were, he was taken aback when the slope unfolded almost at his very feet. Quite by accident, he had put himself at the very brink of the ridge.

Tall Bear was quick to capitalize. Stepping in front of Fargo to prevent him from correcting his mistake, the warrior wove a glittering web in the air, slowly moving closer and closer, trying to back Fargo onto the slope so he would be at an even greater disadvantage.

Fargo let the Ute think the ploy had worked. He retreated, but as he backed down the slope he suddenly hurled himself at Tall Bear's legs.

Too late, Tall Bear bent to block the blow. The razor edge of the toothpick seared into his left shin, glanced off the bone, and pierced his calf. Howling in fury, he sprang into the clear. Blood poured, coating his ankle and foot. He limped to one side, gnashing his teeth, whether in pain or rage it was hard to say.

Unseen by anyone, Fargo reversed his grip on the Arkansas toothpick. Holding it behind him by the tip, he grinned up at the tall warrior. He did not need to say anything. His mocking expression said it all.

Tall Bear was beside himself. Whipping the big knife overhead, he charged, favoring his wounded leg but still moving fast enough to bowl Fargo over by the sheer force of his size and speed.

Only Fargo had no intention of letting his foe get that close. The very second that the tall figure was outlined against the starry background above, he threw the toothpick with all the power his sinews could muster. Steel flashed. Tall Bear jerked, stopped dead, did a slow swivel toward the other warriors, and sank to the grass like a deflated balloon.

Fargo stepped up to the twitching body. Gripping the knife's hilt, he yanked it free and wiped the scarlet blade on the Ute's leggings. "This one is for Morning Flower," he said softly to himself.

A guttural cough reminded Fargo that he wasn't alone. He whirled. The members of the war party were staring at him. In the dark Fargo could not read the expressions in their eyes. He had no way of knowing if they would turn on him or whether they would honor their words and go their way in peace.

The burly Ute stepped forward. His face a blank slate, he regarded the fallen form at his feet. "You good fighter, white man," he said, and smirked. "Maybe you part Ute, eh?" He lifted his arm. It was a signal for others to come forward and bear the body of Tall Bear down the mountain. The rest filed off, gathering their dead as they descended.

One of them jabbed a lance into the stricken horse, finally ending its suffering.

In less than two minutes, Skye Fargo was alone on the ridge. Nothing moved, except the wind stirring his hair. The war party had melted into the night. Only then did it dawn on him that he had never asked the burly Ute's name.

Sudden exhaustion claimed Fargo as he shuffled to the stallion. Part of him wanted to mount up and head out after the widow and the prospector, but he knew this would be foolish. In the past two days he had not slept a single wink. More than anything else, he needed reset.

Right there Fargo spread out his bedroll. He was asleep the second he closed his eyes, and he did not open them again until bright sunshine awakened him in the middle of the morning.

Refreshed, Fargo rode westward. At the top of Wolf Creek Pass he picked up the trail of a lone horse and followed it to the northwest. He couldn't wait to tell Morning Flower the good news.

Shortly before noon Fargo started to cross a valley and spied a large dead animal ahead, partially hidden by tall grass. His gut churning, he galloped over. It was the mount Morning Flower had been riding, with four bullet holes in its side. Someone had shot it out from under her.

Tracks made by shod horses told Fargo the whole story. Just when he thought the lovely Ute was safe, just when things were going in her favor, she'd had the worst stroke of luck of all.

Morning Flower and Ike McDermott were in the clutches of Wolf Rollins.

14

Perched on a thick limb partway up a pine tree, Skye Fargo counted eight horses ground-hitched near the entrance to the cavern on Treasure Mountain. He also saw Morning Flower. Her wrists were bound behind her back, and she sat on a boulder with her slender shoulders slumped in despair. Guarding her was a hard case Fargo remembered from Pagosa Springs.

Fess Webster, his wrist still bandaged, was rolling himself a cigarette.

In an hour or so the sun would set. Fargo knew it was best to wait for the cover of darkness before moving in closer, but he was worried about what might happen to Morning Flower in the meantime. There could only be one reason Wolf Rollins had brought her along. The cutthroats intended to treat themselves to her charms, probably just as soon as they were done gloating over how rich they now were.

As Fargo watched, two laughing killers strolled into the open. One was Bob Hackett, the man who had dropped the noose over Fargo outside the saloon. Both men held silver flasks. Hackett passed his to Webster, who took a long swig.

Good, Fargo reflected. They were celebrating. The alcohol would dull their senses.

Wrapping an arm around the trunk, Fargo shimmied downward. Near the bottom he gripped a limb, swung in a lithe arc down to the next, then dropped to the last branch, hanging a few moments before he let go. The Ovaro gave a low snort as he landed beside it. Claiming the Henry, he crammed extra ammunition into his pockets before stalking toward the cliff.

When Fargo ran out of trees and brush to use for cover, he relied on boulders. Where there were none, he hugged the ground, slipping into ruts or other shallow depressions. He made it a point to hold the Henry close to his side so the shiny brass receiver would not reflect any sunlight and give him away.

Not that the killers would have noticed. Webster, Hackett and their pard were too busy guzzling whiskey and amusing themselves.

Soon Fargo was close enough to hear what they were saying. Webster was telling the others how he planned to take his share and go to New Orleans to set up his very own whorehouse.

"—see it now!" the man gloated. "Every night I'll bed me a different whore. And they'll all be young and pretty and as sweet as honey. Only the best in my place, yessiree!"

Bob Hackett wiped his mouth with his sleeve, stepped up to Morning Flower, and roughly ran a hand over her cheek. "All this talk about females is putting me in the mood. How about it, squaw? Care to have me give you a tumble?"

Morning Flower recoiled. Hackett, chuckling, tried to stroke her hair. She suddenly bent and bit down on his wrist, eliciting a howl. Sinking her teeth in deep, Morning Flower tossed her head as if she were a she-wolf ripping into her prey.

Hackett tried to pull free but couldn't. "You stinking bitch!" Incensed, he drew back his fist. "Let go of me or else!"

Fargo, prone next to a boulder, took aim, but someone else stepped in before he could squeeze the trigger.

"Enough!"

The word cracked like a gunshot. All three hardcases started and glanced around.

Bob Hackett did not let his blow land. Morning Flower opened her mouth and he quickly stepped away from her, blurting, "Boss!"

Lightning danced in Wolf Rollins's eyes. His hands were

poised close to his ivory-handled Colts. "I can't turn my back on any of you idiots for two seconds, can I? When I said that she was to be left alone, I meant it!"

Behind him stood another member of the gang, holding a Spencer trained on Ike McDermott. The prospector was a study in misery, his right cheek split open, his jaw bruised, dried blood under his nose. He gazed forlornly at the Ute woman.

Hackett nervously licked his lips. "I was only having a little fun. She had no call to try and bite my hand off."

Wolf Rollins took a few steps to the right. It gave him a clear shot at Bob Hackett, and no one was more aware of that fact than Hackett himself.

"Now hold on!" the killer declared. "I never meant the bitch any harm. Fess and Sam will back me up on that."

Wolf glanced at Webster and the other gunman, both of whom looked as if they wanted to crawl inside their own skins and hide. Neither spoke in Hackett's defense. Sighing, Wolf faced him squarely. "What do you take me for, Bob? I saw you with my own eyes. You were going to hit her." He paused. "Fill your hand whenever you're ready. Who knows? You might get lucky."

Bob Hackett blanched and began to back off. "Please, Wolf. Don't do this. If you want to be rid of me, just let me have my share of the silver and I'll go."

"You no longer have a share," Wolf Rollins snapped. "We'll split it seven ways instead of eight. The boys will be grateful. It means more for them."

Greed brought smiles to the other gunmen.

Fargo never really expected Hackett to slap leather. The man didn't have a prayer, and had to know it. Maybe desperation goaded him into going for his six-gun. Maybe it was the thought of losing all his newfound wealth. Whatever the case, Bob Hackett swooped a hand to the butt of his Remington and began to draw.

Morning Flower, it turned out, had been right.

The man called Wolf Rollins was incredibly, unbelievably fast. Those twin nickel-plated Colts materialized as if out of thin air. They blasted simultaneously. Bob Hackett was crumpled in half and flung to the ground, neat holes where the pupils of his eyes had been. He convulsed once and was still.

No one else moved. Fess Webster, Hackett's friend, coughed to clear his throat. "I reckon Bob had that coming."

From out of the cavern poured the rest of the outlaws, their pistols drawn. At the sight of their leader holding his smoking Colts, they stopped in their tracks.

Wolf Rollins swung toward them. His hands blurred, and just like that his pistols were sheathed in their holsters. He jabbed a finger at the body. "Anyone else feel inclined to give me a hard time?"

Although they outnumbered him four to one and had their revolvers out, not one man there spoke up.

Wolf pointed at Ike McDermott. "You all heard me give this runt my word. I promised him the squaw wouldn't be harmed if he would lead us to his claim. And he has." He hitched up his crossed gunbelts. "Hackett decided my word wasn't good enough for him. So I gave him his chance and he took it."

"No need to explain yourself to us, boss," a lean drink of water commented.

Fargo stared at Ike McDermott. The prospector had sacrificed everything to spare Morning Flower. It was added proof, if any was needed, that McDermott cared more deeply for her than he had ever been willing to admit.

"Are you saying that we're just going to let the squaw go?" Fess Webster asked Rollins. "What if she talks?"

"Who would she tell?" Wolf growled. "There's no law in these parts. She can't hurt us in any way."

To the amazement of everyone, including Fargo, Morning Flower disagreed. "Yes, I can," she said. "If you do not do as I want, I will ride to Denver. My Joe told me there are Army troops there."

Wolf Rollins reared over her. "Some people don't know when they're well off. I don't like being threatened, squaw! Ever!" He put a finger under her chin and tilted her head higher. "Besides, you're in no position to be making demands."

Ignoring him, Morning Flower demanded, "You must let Ike McDermott go also."

"No can do, Injun," Wolf responded. "We need him to help mine the silver. He's the one with all the prospecting experience. And he's an old hand at blasting with black powder. Those kegs he has stored in there will get the job done in no time."

Morning Flower jerked away from his hand. "I will not leave without him!" she said defiantly.

"You must!" This came from McDermott, who took a step toward her but was gripped by one of the gunmen. "I can't bear the thought of anything happening to you. Please, my dear, for my sake, go while you can. I'm done for, but I want you to get out of this alive."

All eyes were on the woman. No one noticed as Fargo rose high enough to prop an elbow on the boulder and steady his sights on Wolf Rollins. "We both do," he said.

The outlaws spun, several extending their revolvers. Their leader glued them in place with a surly command. "No firing, damn it, or you'll answer to me!"

Fargo met Wolf Rollin's fiery gaze over the barrel of the Henry. The two-gun killer knew that he'd be the first to take lead if any of his men got an itchy trigger finger.

Wolf did not act flustered in the least. Nodding at the widow and the prospector, he said. "They told us you were dead."

Fargo was not going to allow Rollins to distract him with meaningless talk. "Have your men toss their hardware. Then step back and let McDermott and the woman come toward me."

"You know I can't do that."

"I'll count to three," Fargo said.

A sneer creased the big gunman's lupine features. "You're bluffing. You can't possibly get all of us before we make wolf meat of you."

"One."

Fess Webster anxiously glanced from Fargo to Rollins. "What do we do, boss? What do we do?"

"Two," Fargo counted.

Tension crackled in the air. The cutthroats were coiled to

obey their leader. Morning Flower and Ike McDermott were rigid with suspense.

Only Wolf Rollins stayed as calm as if he were at a church social. He actually laughed, then said, "All right, boys. I guess we're licked. We'll have to do as we're told." His men looked at him as if he were loco as he slowly started to shed his fancy Colts, using only his thumb and forefinger on each hand to pluck them from their scabbards.

Fargo had the man covered at a distance of fifteen feet. He did not think someone even as quick on the draw as Wolf Rollins would try to beat a bullet at that range. Yet that was exactly what the man in the black hat did.

Suddenly pivoting and throwing himself to the left, Wolf fired four swift shots. Fargo stroked off one of his own and knew he had missed. Then he had to drop behind the boulder as the rest of the killers cut loose. Slugs whined into space inches above his head, chipping bits of stone that stung him like a swarm of mosquitoes.

Fargo rose up and snapped off another shot. Rollins and the gunmen were backpedaling toward the cavern. One of the outlaws was dragging Ike McDermott by the arm. The feisty prospector kicked and twisted but he couldn't break the man's grip.

Morning Flower had thrown herself to the ground at the first shot and had her nose pressed against the earth to keep from being caught in the cross fire.

Rolling to the left, Fargo pushed himself up on his knees. He had time for one more shot before the gang reached cover, and he aimed at the gunman dragging McDermott. But at the exact instant that he squeezed the trigger, another outlaw stepped into his sights and took the slug instead. The man crumpled. Fargo hastily compensated, but to no avail.

The gunmen reached the mouth of the tunnel. At a bellow from Wolf Rollins, they stopped spraying lead.

On hands and knees Fargo hustled over to Morning Flower. Tears of joy rimmed her eyes as he flourished the toothpick.

"I was so afraid I would never see you again!"

"You had me confused with Tall Bear," Fargo said. The

hemp parted, and she turned to throw her arms around him. A warm teardrop trickled down his neck. "Save this for later," he cautioned huskily. "We're not out of the woods yet."

Morning Flower nodded and dabbed at an eye. "We must get Ike out of there."

But how? Fargo wondered. From where he knelt, he could see the cavern entrance clearly. None of the outlaws were fool enough to show themselves. And why should they? All they had to do was wait until the sun went down, then come out in force. Cupping a hand to his mouth, he hollered, "Rollins! Can you hear me?"

"What do you want?" was the immediate reply.

"Send McDermott out and we'll go our way in peace," Fargo proposed.

The gunman's gruff laughter echoed hollowly in the tunnel. "You must take me for the biggest jackass who ever lived! The runt is back in the cavern, and that's where he'll stay. He's too valuable to us."

Morning Flower, scowling, started to jump up in plain sight of the gunmen, heedless of the peril.

Seizing her by the wrist, Fargo pulled her back down. "Getting yourself killed won't help McDermott any."

"I wish you had seen him after they caught us," Morning Flower said, gazing sadly at the cavern. "He was so brave! They beat him, they kicked him, they tossed him from one to the other. But Ike would not tell them where to find the ore." She sniffled. "Then Wolf Rollins said he would do the same to me if Ike did not do as they wanted. So Ike agreed to bring them here." Her voice choked off. "Why did I not see how he feels sooner?"

It was a question that did not need an answer. Fargo glanced at the eight horses and had a brainstorm that would keep her busy and help take her mind off the prospector for a while. "Think you can sneak on over there and start leading their mounts into the trees while I cover you?"

"What?" Morning Flower said, blinking back more tears. She faced the animals. "Oh. Yes. I can." Quickly lying on her belly, she crawled off.

Fargo watched the entrance closely as she worked from

boulder to boulder. He hoped the outlaws were too busy talking over what they were going to do to notice her.

Morning Flower's Ute heritage showed itself. As if she were raiding an enemy village, she noiselessly crept to the farthest horse, calmed it by rubbing its neck, then guided it into the undergrowth, never once showing herself to the killers. In moments she was back for the next horse. Then another. Not a one gave her any trouble until the fourth nipped at her hand and would not let her grab the reins. She had to stand to seize them, then tug and cajole to get the animal into the trees.

Fargo thought he saw movement in the cavern, but no targets presented themselves. He noted the position of the setting sun, gauging they had about half an hour of daylight left.

Presently only a single mount remained. Morning Flower took hold of the reins and rotated to lead it off. The bay was temperamental. Nickering loudly, it stepped a few yards closer to the cavern.

"What the hell?" someone cried. "They're stealing our horses!"

A gunman hurtled into the open, his pistol lining up with Morning Flower's chest. Fargo was not caught napping. His slug penetrated the killer below the arm and exited at the right shoulder blade, spewing blood and bone and gore everywhere.

Others charged out. Fargo levered the Henry again and again, blistering them, driving them back into the cavern, one with a busted arm, another with a crimson stain on one leg. They vented their wrath in a string of curses.

Morning Flower was still striving to lead the last horse off into the forest. The animal foiled her at every turn, digging in its hooves when she hauled on the reins and whipping its head from side to side when she attempted to snatch the bridle.

"Leave it!" Fargo urged. So far she had kept the horse between herself and the cavern, but a lucky shot might drop her. She suddenly turned her back to the animal, threw her shoulder against the reins, and chugged her legs like a steam engine on a steep grade.

A rifle poked from the tunnel mouth. It spat lead and smoke, kicking up dust close to Morning Flower.

Fargo couldn't see the shooter so he shot at the rifle. His second round hit the barrel, tearing the gun from the outlaw's hands. More curses were flung his way.

And still Morning Flower persisted in her struggle with the horse. Puffing and heaving, she had thrown her entire weight into it.

Fargo was about to rush over and drag her back when the bay yielded. As meekly as a tame kitten it followed her toward the trees. She had the presence of mind to hug its side in case the outlaws opened fire, which they did when she had gone barely four feet. They shot at her legs, which were visible under the horse.

To discourage them, Fargo fired at the inner wall of the tunnel. The ping of ricochets mingled with howls of boiling rage. When they stopped shooting, so did he. In the ensuing silence, he saw that Morning Flower had made it to safety. He reloaded, uncertain what the killers would try next. To his surprise, Wolf Rollins hailed him, so he responded. "What do you want?"

"You're a dead man. You know that, don't you?"

"Could be," Fargo called out, "but I'm not the one stranded on foot in the middle of Ute country. You know how fond they are of you."

The outlaw leader did not sound fazed. "Have your fun, mister. It's only a matter of time. If you get away today, I'll come after you and hunt you down."

"Anytime," Fargo said, edging around the boulder so he could see the entrance more clearly. "But in the meantime, what would you say to a swap?"

"Let me guess. The runt for our horses. Is that the deal?"

"That's it. We'll leave them tied in the trees."

"You expect me to take your word for it?" Wolf Rollins said sarcastically.

"I'd take yours."

For a while there was no response. Fargo began to think he had wasted his time and nearly gotten Morning Flower killed for nothing. At last an answer wafted out.

"I'm flattered. Honestly I am. But it's no dice, *hombre*.

We still have numbers on our side, and in about ten seconds we're fixing to bust out of here and gun you down. You won't stand a—"

Unexpectedly, a commotion broke out in the tunnel. There were shouts of, "Boss! Boss!" Someone mentioned McDermott by name, and Fargo caught part of a yell, something to do with a keg of powder. Out of the corner of his eye he saw Morning Flower sprint toward the opening, screaming at the top of her lungs, "No, Ike! No! Don't do it!" He rose to intercept her.

Without warning, a nearly deafening explosion rocked the mountain. The slope heaved and buckled. The ground under Fargo's feet seemed to lift him into the air and settle again. He had barely straightened when a tremendous gust of hot air, dust, and debris gushed out of the tunnel with hurricane force, picking him up and hurling him backward as if he were a child's doll. He spun head over heels, out of control, unsure which way was up and which was down. Dust blinded him, choked him, caked him all over. Somewhere a man shrieked. Then the ground leaped up to meet him and all the breath was slammed from his lungs.

Stunned, Fargo tried to stand. His legs were spongy, his chest ached with every breath. A thick cloud of dust swirled about him, so thick he was unable to see more than a few feet in any direction. Nor could he tell where the cavern lay. He shuffled a few steps, steadied himself, and covered his mouth. By a miracle, he had the Henry in his left hand.

A loud rattling attended the blast, as if a lot of loose dirt and stones were sliding down from above. Fargo slowed, leery of blundering into the path of an avalanche.

Out of the dust materialized a stumbling figure, stooped over. "Morning Flower?" Fargo asid.

The figure snapped erect, coughing violently. At that moment the dust parted, revealing Wolf Rollins. The gunman's broad-brimmed black hat was gone, his shirt and pants in tatters. Dirt covered every square inch of skin and clothing. As the fit subsided, he cracked a grin. "Imagine this. Just the two of us left, and soon there will be only one." With that, he went for his pistols.

Fargo flashed his right hand to his Colt. He saw Wolf Rollins clear leather as he did the same. But his shot boomed a hair ahead of the gunman's. Wolf Rollins staggered. Again Fargo fired, the slug thudding dead center into the killer's torso, jolting the big man with the fancy hardware. Wolf teetered, cast a look of stupefied disbelief at Fargo, and crashed onto his back.

Seconds passed. Fargo stood there, staring at the man who had been the terror of the San Juans. Loud weeping drew him out of himself, and he strode forward, swatting at tendrils of dust. Soon he came to where the cavern entrance had been. It was completely filled in. The blast had brought the roof of the cavern down on top of all those inside, crushing them under countless tons of earth.

Morning Flower was on her knees, vainly clawing at the dirt. She looked up, her cheeks glistening, and said softly, "Ike told me not to worry. On our way here he whispered that he knew how to take care of them." The tears became a flood.

"He was a bigger man than most realized," Fargo said. Shoving the Colt into his holster, he took her by the elbow. It was a long ride to Colorow's village. Maybe by then he could help her forget the hurt. Maybe by then they would be ready to get on with their lives, to leave the memory of Treasure Mountain behind them.

Maybe.

LOOKING FORWARD!
The following is the opening
section from the next novel in the exciting
Trailsman **series from Signet:**

THE TRAILSMAN #178
APACHE ARROWS

1860, southeastern Arizona territory, where an Apache mountain sanctuary promised certain death for any white-eyes who dared to intrude . . .

Rippling waves of blistering heat rose from the desert. To the tall rider making his solitary way across the baked landscape, it was if he were being roasted alive in an oven. Beads of sweat trickled down his brow. Raising a callused hand, he wiped a sleeve across his stinging eyes, then peered out from under his hat brim at the foothills ahead.

Skye Fargo was glad to be alive. The trek across the Chihuahuan Desert had taxed him to his limit, just as it had his prized pinto stallion. The sight of trees and grass was enough to make his heart leap for joy. Licking his parched lips, he rose in the stirrups to look for telltale signs of a spring.

Instead, Fargo saw thin tendrils of pale smoke rising beyond the first hill. Instantly he slowed and dropped his right hand to the smooth butt of his Colt. Where there was smoke, there had to be a campfire. And since few whites dared enter that part of the country, Fargo took it for granted that Indians had made the fire. Hostile Indians.

The Chiricahua Mountains and the territory around them were the domain of the dreaded Chiricahua Apaches, most feared of all the Apache tribes. For more years than anyone cared to count, they had raided and plundered to their heart's content, slaying any whites they caught.

So it was small wonder that Fargo headed for the nearest cover. At the base of the low hill he dismounted, gripped the reins, and carefully led the Ovaro upward. Chaparral had replaced the desert shrub. Manzinita screened them until they were shy of the crest, at which point Fargo ground-hitched the stallion and crept high enough to take a peek at what lay on the other side.

For a few seconds Fargo thought that the sun must have fried his brain. Nestled in a shaded nook beside a slender stream was a cabin. Beside it stood a small barn and a chicken coop. In a corral at the rear were several horses. The smoke curled from the cabin's chimney.

"It can't be!" Fargo marveled under his breath. As far as he knew, no whites had been foolish enough to homestead in that region. To do so courted certain death. Yet he couldn't deny the evidence of his own senses.

On a line stretched between the cabin and the barn flapped clothes hung out to dry. As Fargo looked on, the door opened and out walked a vision of loveliness, a striking woman with hair the color of corn silk and a figure that amply filled her homespun dress. Toting a basket, she went to the clothesline and set about taking her laundry down.

Fargo resisted an urge to pinch himself. He wasn't dreaming. The woman and the buildings were really there. Returning to the Ovaro, he forked leather. Rather than go up and over, he worked his way around to a gully that brought him out within a hundred feet of the homesteader. To her credit, she spotted him the second he appeared and promptly vanished inside the cabin. As he came to a stop near the clothesline, she stepped out again. Only this time she held a Spencer leveled at his chest.

"That's far enough, stranger."

Her voice was vocal honey, so sugary sweet that the

mere sound of it sparked cravings in Fargo any bear would appreciate. He raked her curves with a hungry glance, then reminded himself where he was and why he was there. "Howdy, ma'am," he said cordially. "Mind if I get down and stretch my legs?"

"Yes."

Fargo had started to swing off, taking it for granted that she would let him. The metallic click of the Spencer's hammer being thumbed back turned his limbs to ice. "I only want to water my horse," he said.

The woman nodded toward the stream. "Help yourself. There's plenty. Just keep your distance, or else."

Sighing, Fargo settled in the saddle and slowly wheeled the pinto. "Suit yourself, lady," he said. He wasn't about to press the issue. If she wanted her privacy, that was her right. But he couldn't resist commenting, "It's none of my business, but if I were you, I'd pack up everything I own and light a shuck for Tucson. If the Apaches ever find out you're here, you won't last two minutes."

The corners of her full mouth quirked. "How noble of you to be so concerned about someone you don't even know."

Her sarcasm galled Fargo. Sure, she was the kind of woman that would make any man drool, but he really did have her best interests at heart. "Go to hell," he said, and left her standing there with her mouth hanging open.

Like most Arizona waterways at that time of year, the stream was shallow and sluggish, on the verge of drying up. But seldom had any water tasted so delicious as Fargo dipped his face into a pool no bigger than a puddle and drank greedily. Filling his hat, he upended it over his head, grinning as the cool liquid spilled over his buckskins.

The soft tread of a foot alerted Fargo to the fact he was no longer alone. As casual as could be, he dipped his hat into the stream again. Right behind him, gravel crunched. Suddenly shifting, he spun. The woman was there, sure enough, and she had the Spencer trained on his back.

Fargo hurled the contents of his hat into her face, catching her off guard. She recoiled, taking a step backward, but not fast enough to prevent him from grabbing her rifle and wrenching it from her grasp. Before she could clear her eyes, he had her own weapon pointed at her trim belly. "I don't take kindly to being filled with lead," he declared.

The woman betrayed no fear. Her tongue flicked out and licked drops from her rosy lips. "If I'd wanted to make buzzard bait of you, mister," she said, "I'd have done it the moment you showed."

Fargo slowly lowered the Spencer. He prided himself on being a keen judge of character, and he could tell that the beauty meant every word.

"I came over to apologize for being so rude," she explained, "and to ask if you'd like a cup of coffee. I have a fresh pot on the stove."

Among the clothes on the line were a man's shirt and pants. "Are you sure your husband won't object?" Fargo asked. Having tangled with more than his fair share of jealous spouses, he wanted to avoid any trouble.

"I'm not married," the woman said, and let it go at that. Extending her hand, she added, "Let's start over. I'm Cassandra Fletcher. Most folks just call me Cassie."

She had a warm, firm shake. Introducing himself, Fargo gave back her rifle. "I meant what I told you about getting out of here," he stressed. "Apache country is no place for any sane person to put down roots."

Cassie regarded the homestead sadly. "You're not telling me anything I don't already know. Were it up to me, I'd be living in a big city somewhere. St. Louis, maybe, or Memphis. There a body can go to bed at night not wondering if they'll still be alive come morning." Her sorrow deepened. "But we don't always have a choice about things, do we?"

On that puzzling note, the woman led Fargo to her home. He hitched the Ovaro to a crude rail. As he did, he noticed that the cabin itself was an equally crude affair, apparently put up by someone who had no skill at working with wood. The same with the barn and the corral.

Cassie had been watching him. "It's not much," she said, "but it keeps the sidewinders and lizards out."

The interior was cozy. Curtains hung on both windows. A flowered tablecloth covered a small table. The counter and the stove were spotless, and the floor was clean enough to eat off of. Fargo took a seat facing the entrance and rested his forearms in front of him. The fragrance of brewing coffee caused his stomach to rumble.

"Sounds as if you haven't eaten in a spell," Cassie commented while taking a pair of tin cups from a cupboard.

"Not as often as I'd like," Fargo admitted. His pressing business had kept him on the go from dawn until well after dusk, leaving little time to indulge his appetite.

"Want me to fix you some grub?"

The temptation was almost more than Fargo could resist. But he wanted to be deep in the Chiricahuas by nightfall, so he declined. "The coffee will do me just fine."

Cassie filled both cups and sat across from him. Sipping, she openly studied him much as a rancher might study a bull at a cattle auction. "We don't get many people out this way. Leastways, not many whites."

"What else did you expect?" Fargo asked. "Even the army stays away from these mountains." He swallowed, savoring the taste. "I'd bet that if the colonel at Fort Buchanan knew you were here, he'd send in a patrol and have you taken out by force."

"You'd lose that bet," Cassie said. "Colonel O'Neil is well aware of my presence."

Fargo's brow knitted. He found that hard to believe. O'Neil had impressed him as a strict by-the-book officer who wouldn't stand for any nonsense from pesky civilians. Riding herd on the Apaches was hard enough. The last thing O'Neil needed was someone stirring up a hornet's nest by living in the heart of their land. "He hasn't asked you to leave?"

"Dozens of times," Cassie said. "But I can't. So that's that."

Her attitude heightened the mystery. It was as plain as the shapely nose on her lovely face that she'd rather be anywhere other than where she was, yet she stayed on. Why? Fargo wondered.

"And for your information," Cassie Fletcher went on, "O'Neil isn't the only one who knows I'm here. So do the Apaches. Cochise and others stop by from time to time."

In the act of downing more coffee, Fargo paused.

Cochise was a Chiricahua notorious for his dislike of whites. Fargo believed it so highly unlikely the warrior would allow Fletcher to stay there that he was inclined to brand her a liar. Yet her demeanor, and his gut instinct, confirmed her words. "How is it that none of them have taken you for a wife?"

"They don't want to die."

More perplexed than ever, Fargo finished off his cup. It occurred to him that if she were indeed telling the truth, she might be of help to him in his quest. "You must know some of the Apaches personally, then?"

Cassie averted her eyes. "A few."

"Ever heard of a warrior named Nah-tanh?"

"Why?"

Fargo debated whether to tell her. If she was friendly with the Chiricahuas, she might see fit to warn them that he was in the area. The decision was taken from his hands by the abrupt patter of feet outside. Straightening, he made a stab for his pistol but checked his draw when the doorway framed a boy of eleven or twelve who barked excited statements in a language Fargo had last heard on a previous visit to the Arizona Territory. It was the Chiricahua tongue.

The youngster looked to be Indian. From head to toe he was dressed as a Chiricahua warrior would be, in a long-sleeved shirt, pants, a breechcloth, and high moccasins unique to the Apaches. A headband enclosed his hair. At his side hung a long butcher knife in a studded Apache sheath. But his features, while bronzed dark by the sun, were clearly the features of a white boy. As were his hazel eyes. And his hair, although worn in typical Apache fashion, was sandy, not raven black as a true Apache's always was.

The boy was a half-breed, Fargo realized. When Cassie Fletcher turned and answered in the same tongue, it dawned on Fargo who the boy's mother must be, and suddenly he saw the woman in a whole new light.

"My son says we are about to have visitors," Cassie translated urgently. "You must hide until they go away."

Fargo didn't waste precious time asking questions. He was out the door and to the Ovaro in a twinkling. The boy leaped back, as if afraid Fargo would strike him, then observed Fargo's every move as he unwound the reins and hastened around the far corner.

Along the west side of the cabin grew a stand of cottonwoods bordered by brush. Fargo took the stallion into the very heart of the growth. Covering its muzzle to keep it from nickering and giving him away, he stared through a narrow gap in the trees. Cassie and the boy had stepped to the clothesline. Hardly had she removed the first garment than there was movement across the clearing. As if from out of thin air, a dozen or so swarthy figures had materialized.

Fargo recognized one of them right away, even though he had never set eyes on the man before. The warrior was a giant. An iron frame sheathed by corded sinews and muscles carried the newcomer to the middle of the clearing. An enormously broad head warily swung from side to side. At a gesture from him, the rest fanned out.

It was none other than Mangus Colorado, chief of the Mimbreno Apaches and close friend to Cochise. Fargo's mouth went as dry as it had been before he slaked his thirst. Of all the Apaches, Mangus Colorado had a reputation for being the most bloodthirsty. For over fifty years the man had waged relentless war against Mexicans and Americans alike.

The Mimbre chief addressed Cassie Fletcher. She answered while going on about the business of removing her wash. Presently she stopped and went inside. When she emerged, she carried a pair of saddlebags. These she gave to Mangus, who accepted them without comment.

As silently as they had appeared, the Mimbres melted into the chaparral. Fargo waited until he was confident they were long gone, then he returned the pinto to the hitch rail. "Thanks for not letting them know where I was," he said as the woman and the boy joined him.

"Mangus likes to pay me a visit when he is on his way back from raids into Mexico," Cassie said. She offered a wan smile. "He has grown quite fond of my jerky, so I always keep a supply on hand. Just in case."

The more Fargo learned, the more amazed he became.

Here this woman was, friendly with the single most dreaded warrior in the entire Southwest. She was friendly, too, with Cochise, and yet she took it all in stride, as if it were the most natural thing in the world. There was much more to Cassandra Fletcher than seemed apparent. He would very much have liked to get to know her better. But he had a job to do.

"We were lucky Mangus didn't spot the tracks you made coming in," she was saying. "If he had, he would have turned my place upside down to find you."

The boy said something in the Chiricahua tongue. His mother pursed her lips, then nodded. "Ish-kay-nay has a point. There might be stragglers, bringing plunder. If they should pass by while you're still around—" She had no need to finish the statement.

Fargo reluctantly mounted. After the kindness they had shown him, he was not about to put their lives in danger. "I'd better be on my way, then," he said, and was surprised when she frowned. He turned the Ovaro to the north.

"You're not thinking of heading deeper into the mountains, are you?" Cassie asked.

"Afraid so," Fargo confirmed.

Cassie impulsively took a step and placed a hand on his leg. "Please don't. Whatever you're after isn't worth your life."

"We don't always have a choice about things," Fargo told her. Once more he went to leave, but she held on.

"You might like to know that the Chiricahuas were on a raid west of here about a week ago. With them and Mangus on the prowl, you'd be smart to lay low for a while."

Fargo already knew about the Chiricahuas. He'd stopped at Fort Buchanan after leaving Tucson and been told of their latest raids. To cut the risk of running into them, he had looped around to the south and approached the Chiricahua Mountains through the Chihuahuan Desert. "I'm obliged for the warning," he said. "If I make it back this way, maybe I'll stop and pay my respects."

"I'd like that," Cassie said. "But you'd better not. The boy's father is due back in a few days, and he'd shoot you on sight."

Fargo couldn't help but note that she didn't refer to the man as her husband. Her tone implied she would rather he never showed up. "I just might take the chance," he said, and touched his hat brim.

Tapping his spurs on the stallion's flanks, Fargo rode into the manzanita. He was alert for the Mimbres or any other recent sign of roving war parties. At the next hill he climbed to a shelf and delayed long enough to gaze back at the homestead. The cabin was a tiny oasis of civilization in the middle of a vast sea of savage wilderness. Smoke still curled from the chimney. "She has no business being there," he informed the Ovaro.

With a shrug Fargo went on. He held the pinto to a walk, as much to keep from raising dust as to conserve the stallion's energy. The temperature had to be somewhere between ninety-five and a hundred. Within a half hour he was parched, his buckskins clinging to his body.

Fargo covered two more miles. Since it was only early afternoon, he had no intention of stopping. But when the pinto commenced to limp, he immediately reined up.

No one lasted long in the Chiricahuas stranded on foot. Quite a few miners, trappers, and traders had lost mounts for one reason or another, and their bleached bones were all that were found of them later on.

The rugged land was as hostile as the Indians who lived in it. As if the searing heat and lack of water were not enough to deal with, there were bears and mountain lions and rattlers and scorpions, any one of which could end a man's life in the blink of an eye. There were prickly plants that could slash a leg or arm wide open. There were rocks as sharp as razors.

So Fargo made it a point to inspect the Ovaro's hoof on the spot. He found a stone wedged fast and pried it out using his Arkansas toothpick. Always strapped around his right ankle in a custom sheath, the throwing knife had saved his hide many times.

Satisfied the pinto was all right, Fargo replaced the toothpick, then grasped the saddle horn, about to climb on. At that very moment, northwest of him, a twig faintly snapped. As he had done at the cabin, he covered the

Ovaro's muzzle and cocked his head, straining to catch other sounds.

There were none. Not for a while. The next noise Fargo heard were muted voices, closer than the twig had been. They were not clear enough for him to make sense of what was being said, but there was no doubt the speakers were Indians. Apaches, most likely. Whether they were Chiricahuas or Mimbres hardly mattered. Either would slay him without a qualm.

That was the Apache way, after all. To kill without being killed, to steal without being caught, those were the virtues valued most highly by every warrior, whether he was a member of those two tribes or a Mescalero, a Jicarilla, a Tonto, or from one of the western bands.

Fargo tensed as the voices came steadily nearer. A pair of vague forms moved through the brush, bearing to the southwest. With a little luck, he reflected, they would pass within thirty feet of him and never realize he was there. He barely breathed as the two warriors came to an unexpected halt. They seemed to be bent over, examining the ground.

A fly perched on top of the Ovaro's nose, and the stallion tried to toss its head. Fargo held on tight. The stallion, undaunted, tried again. It took every ounce of Fargo's strength to keep the animal still. He saw the fly take to the air, buzz overhead in a wide circle, then land above the pinto's eye. The horse blinked, attempted to shake the pest off, and when that failed, stomped a hoof.

Both Apaches uncoiled.

Another few seconds and Fargo would have been safe. Every nerve on fire, he braced for an outcry and the blast of a rifle or the zing of a feathered shaft. None came. The pair looked to the east awhile, then resumed their journey.

Fargo let out his breath, too soon. The fly had flown off but it did not go far. It alighted on the very same spot above the stallion's eye.

The Ovaro had had enough. Prancing sideways, the pinto almost yanked Fargo off his feet. Fargo lost part of his grip and lunged to reclaim it, but the damage had been done. The stallion jerked its head from side to side and let out with a whinny.

Fargo had to get out of there. Vaulting onto the saddle, he bent low and moved off at a brisk walk. Any faster, and the heavy thud of hooves would enable the Apaches to pinpoint him. He skirted a thicket and twisted.

As quietly as ghosts, the warriors had raced back but had not yet spotted him. They were concentrating on dense brush south of him. Suddenly both dropped from sight, as if swallowed by the earth.

Fargo had no idea what to make of it. Since they were much too close, he stopped, counting on the thicket to conceal him. For all of fifteen seconds nothing happened. He suspected that they already knew where he was and were closing in. Edging his spurs backward, he was set to gallop off when both warriors popped up again twenty feet from the place they had gone to ground.

Fargo was puzzled when they dived into high weeds and a struggle ensued. They were grappling with someone who put up quite a tussle. There would never be a better chance for Fargo to slip away, but he stayed there to see who they had jumped. He figured it must be another Indian, maybe a Pima or Maricopa, mortal enemies of the Apaches. Then the pair stepped into view holding a squirming captive between them.

It was Cassie Fletcher's son.

SAVAGE

FRONTIER

by Frank Burleson

1854. In the East, tension between North and South pulled the country apart, with a weak President helpless to stop it and Secretary of War Jefferson Davis following his own agenda. But in the West, a different threat arose. A new generation of Apache leaders were taking over, who would no longer talk peace with the White Eyes. Instead they would fight with the courage, daring, and brilliance that was the Apache pride.

First Lieutenant Nathanial Barrington was already a battle-scarred veteran of the Apache Wars. But nothing in his passion-driven life as a man and fighting life as a soldier prepared him for the love that flamed in the shadow of the gathering storm—or for the violence sweeping over the Southwest in the greatest test the U.S. Army ever faced and the hardest choice Barrington ever had to make. . . .

from SIGNET

WHISPERS OF THE MOUNTAIN
BY TOM HRON

The Indians of Alaska gave the name Denali to the great sacred mountain they said would protect them from anyone who tried to take the vast wilderness from them. But now white men had come to Denali, looking for the vast lode of gold that legend said was hidden on its heights. A shaman lay dead at the hands of a greed-mad murderer, his wife was captive to this human monster, and his little daughter braved the frozen wasteland to seek help. What she found was lawman Eli Bonnet, who dealt out justice with his gun, and Hannah, a woman as savvy a survivor as any man. Now in the deadly depth of winter, a new hunt began on the treacherous slopes of Denali—not for gold but for the most dangerous game of all....

from **SIGNET**

PROMISED LAND
Jason Manning

Legendary mountain man Hugh Falconer was not free to choose where to go as he led a wagon train he had saved from slaughter at the hands of a white renegade, a half-breed killer, and a marauding Pawnee war party. Falconer took the people he was sworn to protect, and a woman he could not help wanting, into a secluded valley to survive until spring.

But there was one flaw in his plan that turned this safe haven into a terror trap. A man was there before them ... a man who ruled the valley as his private kingdom ... a mountain man whose prowess matched Falconer's own ... a man with whom Falconer had to strike a devil's bargain to avoid a bloodbath ... or else fight no-holds-barred to the death ... or both. ...

from **SIGNET**

*Prices slightly higher in Canada.   (0-451-186478—$5.99)